Marin froze at the sound of the front door opening, then slamming shut, followed by a swift and undoubtedly masculine tread approaching down the hallway

Sick with fright, she looked around for something—anything—that she could use to defend herself against the intruder.

Except that he was already in the doorway, his voice harsh with irritation as he demanded, "For God's sake, Lynne, have you suddenly gone deaf?" and paused, with a swift intake of breath, as realization dawned.

Marin found herself being comprehensively surveyed by eyes as glacially blue as a polar sea. When he spoke again, his voice was ominously quiet. "Who the hell are you, and what are you doing here?"

Obeying an instinct she barely understood, she made sure the folds of her towel were secure.

"I could ask you the same thing," she retorted, her voice quivering a little because she already knew the answer. That the unexpected and unwanted visitor, looking her over as she stood there, next door to naked and embarrassed out of her life, was Lynne's boss, Jake Radley-Smith.

"Don't play games, sweetheart," he advised, his tone as cold as his gaze….

All about the author…
Sara Craven

SARA CRAVEN was born in South Devon, England, and grew up in a house full of books. She worked as a local journalist, covering everything from flower shows to murders, and started writing for Harlequin in 1975. When not writing, she enjoys films, music, theater, cooking and eating in good restaurants. She now lives near her family in Warwickshire. Sara has appeared as a contestant on the former U.K. game show *Fifteen to One,* and in 1997 was the television *Mastermind* champion. In 2005 she was a member of the Romantic Novelists' team on *University Challenge—the Professionals.*

Sara Craven

HIS UNTAMED INNOCENT

TORONTO • NEW YORK • LONDON
AMSTERDAM • PARIS • SYDNEY • HAMBURG
STOCKHOLM • ATHENS • TOKYO • MILAN • MADRID
PRAGUE • WARSAW • BUDAPEST • AUCKLAND

Recycling programs
for this product may
not exist in your area.

ISBN-13: 978-0-373-23725-5

HIS UNTAMED INNOCENT

First North American Publication 2010.

Printed in U.S.A.

HIS UNTAMED INNOCENT

CHAPTER ONE

THEY SAID THE only sure things in life were death and taxes, Marin Wade thought as she lifted the sponge and squeezed wonderfully warm, scented water over her shoulders and down her breasts. But there was an additional certainty— that as soon as you got into a hot and longed-for bath the phone would ring.

Just as it was doing at this very moment.

Yet for once she would not be scrambling out, cursing and reaching for a towel in order to obey its summons because—oh joy, oh bliss—it was not her phone.

Whoever it was at the other end could speak to the answering machine.

Of course, it might be Lynne calling to check that she was settling in and that all was well, but if so she'd leave a message too. And later, when Marin was bathed and fed, she'd ring back and thank her stepsister yet again for offering her this temporary bolt hole with so few questions asked. Up to now, at least, she thought wryly.

Lynne was three years her senior, and since their parents had retired to a villa beside a golf course in Portugal she'd taken her elder-sister role very seriously indeed. So when she returned on Sunday night she'd want to know why Marin's dream job had come to a premature end.

And by then it might be good to have someone to confide in over the entire nasty mess.

Because she would be starting to feel better about it all. Once she'd got over her tiredness and the chaos of the last twenty-four hours and could think straight, she'd have this whole weekend to herself to start making plans and being positive about her life, rather than wanting to howl.

Of course, she'd have to wait until Monday to find out if she still had a job with the agency, or if her erstwhile employer's threat to have her fired had born fruit, she thought unhappily. But at least she could start looking for somewhere to live until her own flat became available again.

Not that it wasn't gorgeous here. Lynne had told her she was welcome to stay as long as she wanted, but she needed to stand on her own two feet and get herself together again as soon as possible.

She looked around her almost in awe. This bathroom alone was to-die-for, she thought; its soft, aqua tiles made you imagine that you were floating in some warm, foreign sea. Add to that the spacious living room with its raised dining-alcove, the state-of-the-art kitchen and the two elegantly fitted bedrooms, and Marin was as near to living in the lap of luxury as she was ever likely to get.

What she couldn't quite figure was how Lynne could possibly afford such a sumptuous environment.

Her stepsister was, of course, the personal assistant of Jake Radley-Smith, principal of one of the most successful financial public-relations firms in the UK—but surely she'd have to be earning mega-bucks in order to rent even a cupboard in a place like this?

Although Marin was wallowing in it all, she felt vaguely uneasy just the same, knowing how extremely ordinary Lynne's previous flat had been.

And, if she hadn't known that Lynne was deeply in love with Mike and on her way to Kent with him this very minute to meet his parents, she might even be wondering what kind of 'personal assistance' her stepsister had actually provided for her high-flying boss, and whether this flat was payment for services rendered.

As if, she thought, pulling a face at herself. Dirt must be catching.

She leaned back against the quilted head-rest, closing her eyes, as she contemplated the disastrous turn her life had taken. The worst of it was, she hadn't seen it coming. Which must make her the biggest, most naïve idiot still walking free.

It had also been stupid to agree to a short-term let of her own flat during her absence, but hindsight was a wonderful thing, and the position she'd been

offered with best-selling romantic novelist Adela
Mason had been guaranteed for a minimum of six
months, so it had seemed safe enough at the time.

'Her usual secretary has to have time off. Her
elderly mother is about to have a serious operation
and will need a lot of after-care,' her boss Wendy
Ingram had told her. 'Ms Mason does her research
in London, then goes down to her house in south-
western France to do the actual writing, so she wants
someone to fill the gap.' She had pursed her lips. 'Apparently, we were recommended to her, but she's
not easy to please.'

'Adela Mason,' Marin had echoed, her hazel eyes
shining. 'I can't believe it. She's a terrific writer.
I'm her number one fan.'

'Which is why I suggested you, although I suspect
you're rather too young. But she's already turned
down Naomi and Lorna, and says she wants
someone *simpatico,*' Wendy had snorted. 'But don't
allow your enthusiasm for her as an author to run
away with you,' she'd added dourly. 'You may be
sick of the sight of the new book before it's finished.
I looked her up on the Internet and saw this magazine
interview with her. She writes in longhand, it seems,
on special paper with a special pen. You'll be typing
the drafts on to a computer for her to correct, and
there could be as many as ten of them.'

She paused. 'You'll also be doing a lot of fetching
and carrying as well; being her secretary will only
be part of it. She's looking for a one-woman service

industry, and you'll be earning every cent she pays you. But as she's just remarried you may at least be spared from bringing her the cup of designer hot-chocolate she likes last thing at night.'

'For a chance to work with Adela Mason, I'd even pick the cocoa beans,' Marin assured her jubilantly. 'It's not a problem.'

'But getting through the interview might be,' Wendy warned.

Adela Mason had been taking part in a TV panel game that evening, dark hair cut in a severe bob, and a crimson dress making the most of an enviable figure. She was bright and sparky, and had emerged as an easy winner, accepting the plaudits of her fellow-panellists with apparent modesty.

Yet there had been something about her smile and the turn of her head that had plainly been intended to remind them all that she was also the biggest earner on the show.

Why should that worry me? Marin had asked herself. *I'm not going to be any kind of rival, just a toiler in her vineyard—if I get through the interview, that is.*

However, somewhat to her own surprise, she'd done so.

'You seem to have rather more about you than the other candidates,' Ms Mason had told her, playing with the large solitaire-diamond on her wedding finger. 'One of them gave the impression she'd never read a book in her life, and the other was just—unsuitable.' She looked Marin over, taking in the slender body, the light brown hair swept back from her face and fastened at her nape with a ribbon, the pale, creamy skin and quiet, unremarkable features, and nodded. 'Yes, if your keyboard skills are up to scratch, I think you'll do very well.'

She'd paused. 'I'm planning to go down to Evrier sur Tarn next week. I expect you to be available to travel with me. Betsy made all the stopover arrangements before she went off to play Florence Nightingale, but if there are any difficulties I expect you to sort them out.'

Marin could have done without that fairly callous remark about her predecessor, but she'd smiled and agreed that sorting of most kinds was well within her remit.

Not realising that, less than a month later, it would be her own immediate future that would need her attention.

And there, she thought with faint annoyance, went that damned phone again.

'People know I'm away,' Lynne had told her as she'd left, adding drily, 'And I've left Rad a written memo too, so you shouldn't be disturbed.'

Except it wasn't working out like that. Someone or more had clearly slipped through the net.

'Please leave your message after the tone,' she advised the unknown caller in a sing-song voice, before adding more hot water and some extra drops of perfumed oil to the bath and sliding further down into its comforting depths.

It must be lovely, she reflected wistfully, to be so much in demand, to have friends constantly ringing to suggest a cinema, a meal or even a drink.

And to have someone like Mike…

That probably most of all, she admitted. Because, at twenty, she still hadn't had anything approaching a serious relationship with a man.

On the other hand, she was by no means Marin No-Mates. She'd gone on dates since she'd been in London, of course she had, generally making up foursomes with the other girls at the agency. Occasionally, the guy she'd been partnered with for the evening had asked to see her again. Occasionally.

But in all honesty it had never really mattered to her when there had been no further contact.

She was the first to recognise that she was shy and found it difficult to sparkle in company, that she didn't know how to flirt, or take part in the jokey conversations that said one thing but meant something completely different. That she couldn't in a thousand years imagine herself being drawn into the kind of casual intimacy that seemed the norm these days.

Not that she disapproved, exactly. What other people did on the briefest acquaintance was none of her business. She only knew that it wasn't for her, that her own inhibitions weren't so easily discarded. Probably the men she encountered knew it too, and decided to go after girls with fewer hang-ups.

'Do you think I'm a freak?' she'd once asked Lynne, troubled, but the other had only laughed.

'No, honey pie, I think you've got principles and you're going to need to fall very seriously in love before you're tempted to abandon them. And there's nothing remotely freakish about that, so stop beating yourself up.'

The memory of that made Marin smile. Lynne was so good for her, she thought gratefully, so warm and outgoing like her father, Derek Fanshawe, who'd met and fallen in love with Marin's mother six years earlier.

And very different from her own father, who'd been a quiet man, Marin thought, but fond. Her childhood had been safe and comfortable in the shelter of her parents' happy marriage.

Clive Wade had been a successful solicitor, who specialised rather ruefully in divorce, declaring that every case that crossed his desk made him count his own blessings all over again.

And he'd gone on counting them until the day he'd collapsed outside a courtroom and died with terrible suddenness from a heart weakness no one had ever suspected, leaving Marin's smiling, bright-eyed mother as a grey-faced ghost unable to comprehend so devastating a loss.

Looking blankly back at people who told her that at least she had no money worries. That Clive had been a high earner, and had invested shrewdly. And that she should sell their mortgage-free home with its memories and move on.

But it had been three years before a friend, who

worked with her in the charity shop where Barbara
Wade spent most of her mornings, had persuaded her
to join her on a luxury trip round the Norwegian
fjords. Derek Fanshawe, a big man with a ready
smile, had been assigned to their table on the first
evening, and by the time the cruise had ended
Barbara, to her own surprise, no longer felt guilty
about warming to his charm and ebullient kindness.
Realised in fact that she was going to miss him more
than she'd believed possible.

Only to discover he was not prepared to become
a reminiscence to be smiled over and put aside. That,
as a widower with an only daughter, he wanted to see
Barbara again and eventually ask her to make a new
life with him.

There could, Marin realised, have been so many
problems. Second families so often didn't work, and
at first she hadn't wanted to like Derek, seeing this
as disloyalty to her father's memory.

But he'd accepted her dilemma with such understanding and sensitivity that it had been impossible not
to meet him at least halfway. And, watching her
mother bloom in his affection, she'd soon grown to
love him and know that she could welcome their
marriage.

While in Lynne she'd found not only a sister but
a friend. So, in spite of recent events, she could count
her blessings too.

Although the telephone issuing yet another imper-
ative summons was definitely not among them.

Groaning, she leaned forward to let the water drain away, then lifted herself lithely out of the bath, reaching for one of the fluffy, white bath sheets waiting in a neat pile on the tiled surround and wrapping it round her like a sarong, tucking the ends in above her breasts.

She shook her hair loose, combing the damp ends with her fingers, before wandering barefoot down the passage into the living room.

She went to the telephone table and pressed the 'play' button. A man's voice—not Mike's—said abruptly, 'Lynne, pick up. It's urgent.' The second message was simply a sigh, expressing impatience and exasperation in equal measure, and the third had been cut off as soon as the machine had kicked in.

Perhaps the caller had decided it was time to take no for an answer after all, Marin thought as she turned away—then froze as she heard the rattle of a key in a lock, the sound of the front door opening then slamming shut, followed by a swift and un-doubtedly masculine tread approaching down the hallway.

Sick with fright, she looked round for something, anything that she could use to defend herself against the intruder.

Except that he was already in the doorway, his voice harsh with irritation as he demanded, 'For God's sake, Lynne, have you suddenly gone deaf?' He paused with a swift intake of breath as realisation dawned.

Marin found herself being comprehensively surveyed by eyes as glacially blue as a polar sea. When he spoke again, his voice was ominously quiet. 'Who the hell are you, and what are you doing here?'

Obeying an instinct she barely understood, she made sure the folds of the towel were secure.

'I could ask you the same thing,' she retorted, her voice quivering a little, because she already knew the answer—that the unexpected and unwanted visitor looking her over as she stood there, next door to naked and embarrassed out of her life, was Lynne's boss, Jake Radley-Smith.

'Don't play games, sweetheart,' he advised, his tone as cold as his gaze. 'Just answer my questions before I call the police. How did you get in here?'

'I'm staying with my sister.'

'Sister?' he repeated, as if the word was in a foreign language. 'But Lynne's an only child.'

'Stepsister, then,' she said. 'Her father married my mother several years ago.'

'Yes,' he said slowly. 'I'd forgotten. But it doesn't explain why she's given you the run of the place. However, that can wait.' He glanced round, raking a hand through dark hair worn rather longer than fashion dictated. 'So where is Lynne? I need to talk to her urgently.'

'She's not here; she's away for the weekend in Kent. She said she'd told you.'

The tanned face became, if possible, even more

forbidding. 'I thought I might catch her before she left.'

Which was exactly why Lynne had made such a speedy departure, thought Marin.

'I'm not missing out again,' her stepsister had said grimly as she'd fastened her weekend case. 'I'm going before Rad the workaholic finds another pressing reason for me to stay in London, like he did last time I planned to go to Kent. He may be prepared to put in twenty-four-seven, but not everyone feels the same, and I'd rather have this time off than a bonus, however generous, or Mike's parents will wonder if I'm avoiding them.'

Marin straightened her bare shoulders. 'I'm afraid not,' she said. 'She'll be back on Sunday.'

'Which does not solve the problem I have this evening,' Jake Radley-Smith said curtly.

She lifted her chin. 'I quite see she should have stayed here on the off chance you might need her,' she returned with equal crispness. 'But Lynne happens to have a life, and on balance I'd say it's rather more important for her to meet the people who are going to be her in-laws than hang around in order to pander to her employer's last-minute requests.'

There was a silence, then he said, 'Quite a speech, Miss…er…?'

'Wade,' she supplied. 'Marin Wade. And, as you can see for yourself that Lynne isn't here, I'd really like you to go, please.'

He said almost pleasantly, 'I'm sure you would, Miss Wade, but it's hardly for you to order me off my own premises.' The blue eyes looked her over again very much more slowly, and she felt her throat tighten.

It occurred to her that she'd only ever seen him before in newspaper photographs, none of which had done him much justice. He wasn't handsome, she thought, not with that beak of a nose which looked as if it had been broken at some point, but he was more than attractive. Very much more. His eyes were stunning, when they stopped glaring at people, while his mouth...

She stopped right there, telling herself hurriedly that she didn't even want to contemplate his mouth, which had begun to slant into a faint but dangerous smile.

'And you're hardly in any position to throw me out,' he went on softly. 'Not when you're so delightfully undressed. I don't think that towel would stay put for long if it came to a struggle.'

He had her at a total disadvantage, of course. The dark formality of his charcoal business-suit set off the lean virility of his tall body, while the grey brocade waistcoat accentuated his slim waist. His shirt was white and crisp, and his tie was deep-red silk.

He couldn't have been more fully dressed if he'd tried, she thought with bewilderment, so how could he give her the troubling impression that he was exactly the opposite? That, in fact, he wasn't wearing any clothes at all?

She needed to return to safer ground—and fast. She said, dry-mouthed, 'What do you mean—your premises?'

'This is a company flat, Miss Wade,' he drawled, his mouth quirking now in open sensuality. 'It belongs to me, and I use it for foreign clients who don't care for hotels. Lynne is borrowing it, as her landlord, much against his will, is being forced to carry out a major refit of her flat, and all the others in the property. Didn't she explain that before inviting you to move in?'

She shook her head. She said in a small, wooden voice, 'There wasn't much time for explanations. And she didn't know I'd be coming until I rang her from the airport and told her I was pretty much stranded.'

He frowned. 'What happened? Were you robbed on holiday?'

'No, nothing like that. I was working in France, and it—went wrong. And my own place is let for five months.'

'I see,' he said slowly. 'So, that would seem to make you homeless, unemployed and broke.'

'Thank you,' she said, lifting her chin. 'I don't need to have that pointed out to me.'

'Therefore,' he went on as if she hadn't spoken, 'We might be able to do a deal. How much would you charge to spend the evening with me?'

Marin gasped in sheer outrage. 'What do you take me for?' she burst out, then stopped, furiously aware of the response she was inviting.

'Well, clearly not what you're thinking.' He had the audacity to laugh.

'No matter how fetching you may look in that towel—which has slipped a little,' he added softly, 'in case you hadn't noticed.'

Colour stormed into her face as she tugged it hastily back to its former level, cursing his powers of observation.

'And I'm making you a bona fide offer,' he continued. 'I have to go to a party tonight, and the girl I was taking has succumbed to a virus. That's why I called Lynne— because I don't want to turn up at this shindig flying solo, and I'd have paid her over the odds for helping me out. But, as she's not around, you'll do instead.'

There was a taut silence, then she said, 'You have to be joking.'

'Now, there's a stock response,' he commented. 'Your earlier eloquence seems to have deserted you.'

'But not my sense of humour.' She took a deep breath. 'Thank you for your gracious invitation, Mr Radley-Smith, but—no. Not if my life depended on it.'

'I was thinking more of your immediate fiscal future, Miss Wade. Can you really afford to turn down several hundred quid for a couple of hours in my company?'

No, she probably couldn't, she admitted silently, but what difference did that make?

She said, 'I don't belong in your high-powered PR

world, Mr Radley-Smith, believe me. I don't mingle well, I never network and I'm hopeless at parties. Spend your money somewhere else.'

'On the other hand,' he said softly, 'If you obliged me in this, I could be persuaded to turn a blind eye to Lynne's infraction of her tenancy here by taking in waifs and strays. I might even let you stay until your life takes a turn for the better.'

He smiled at her again. 'So, why don't you slip on your little black dress and come with me tonight?'

'Because I do not have a little black dress,' Marin said angrily. 'But I'm sure you have a little black book, Mr Radley-Smith.'

In fact, she knew he had, because Lynne had once told her, laughing that his list of girlfriends was legendary, right up there with the telephone directory. Marin had looked back at her stepsister, so confident and so pretty, and asked, wide-eyed, 'Has he ever made a pass at you?'

Lynne had shrugged. 'Once, in the early days—almost. But never since. I'm not his type—and he certainly isn't mine,' she'd added firmly. 'That's why we work so well together.'

'It's a little late in the day to start ringing round,' he said. He paused, frowning a little. 'Besides, you're an unknown quantity, which suits my purpose far better. So stop arguing, like a good girl, and go and get dressed—black, white or sky-blue pink, I don't care. If you've nothing suitable, borrow from Lynne. You're about the same size, as far as I can judge.'

She could have done without that particular judgement, that lingering blue gaze that seemed to treat her towel as if it had somehow ceased to exist.

'Of course,' he went on more slowly, 'We could always give the party a miss and stay here together instead. There's champagne in the fridge, so we'd be able to relax while you tell me all about yourself, including how you lost your last job.

'And then you wouldn't need to change. You could stay looking as delightful as you do now, give or take an adjustment or two,' he added silkily. 'And subject to negotiation, naturally. Maybe I could persuade you to let that towel slip a little further next time—or even a lot. What do you say?'

'I say,' Marin returned between gritted teeth, aware that she was not only blushing but that her heart was thudding erratically, and resenting him on both counts. 'That on reflection I'd prefer to go to your bloody party.'

His grin made her long to hit him. 'A wise decision, sweetheart. And I'll wait dutifully, if reluctantly, here while you carry out the necessary transformation.' He paused pensively. 'But if you need any help don't hesitate to call me.'

'Count on it,' she said with poisonous sweetness. 'The moment I can think of a name bad enough.'

And, still clutching her towel, Marin beat a strategic if not wholly dignified retreat.

CHAPTER TWO

'I MUST,' MARIN muttered under her breath, 'be completely out of my mind.'

She looked at her reflection with disfavour. Even with the aid of Lynne's cosmetics, she still looked—ordinary. And no one was ever going to believe she was Jake Radley-Smith's girl of choice, even for five minutes, let alone an entire evening.

But at least her favourite dress—a silky, olive-green wraparound, knee-length with cap sleeves, and a long sash that tied on the hip—was wearable. Probably because, unused during her time in France, it had been the last thing she'd taken from the wardrobe and had been packed on top of everything else.

She could only hope it would build her confidence once she had it on, as it usually did. Except that nothing was usual about this particular evening.

She had seriously considered making a dash for it, but Mr Radley-Smith would have seen her passing the living-room door, and she didn't relish the idea of him making a dash for her in return.

Like being stalked by a black panther, she thought with a sudden shiver.

Besides, in practical terms, if she was about to lose her job then she really needed the money he was apparently prepared to pay her for doing him this favour, plus the place to stay. Although the thought of being beholden to him grated on her severely.

The incident in France had been a nightmare, but some instinct she hadn't realised she possessed warned her that any involvement with Jake Radley-Smith had the potential to be infinitely worse.

And she couldn't rely on her lack of glamour to be her safeguard any more, as she'd found to her cost.

She sighed softly, almost despairingly. But some cash in hand would be more than welcome, she reminded herself. In fact, it could be essential.

And, although she might not like parties, she knew what to do at them—grab a soft drink from the tray and become invisible in some corner until it was time to leave.

She was retying her sash in a bow, her fingers having unaccountably turned into thumbs, when he knocked on the door.

'How much longer are you planning to be?'

The dossier was building up nicely, she thought grimly. Too many girlfriends. Far too manipulative. Not enough patience. Plus an excessive amount of—what?—charisma? Sex appeal? She wasn't sure what to call it. Only that she was afraid of it, and would be extra-careful in consequence.

'I'm ready,' she called back, slipping her feet into the waiting high-heeled pewter sandals, and picking up the small bag on its long chain that matched them and her cream-fringed shawl.

She'd expected some comment when she emerged from the bedroom, but he just flicked her with a glance and nodded abruptly.

Not that she wanted his approbation. God forbid. But still…

She said, 'I didn't know what to do with my hair.' She touched its shining fall, reaching, straight as rain water, to her shoulder blades with a self-conscious hand. 'Whether or not I should try to put it up, perhaps.'

'It looks fine.' He walked to the door. 'Shall we go?'

'Whose party is this?' she asked, eventually breaking the silence as she sat beside him in the black cab he'd summoned with such irritating ease. 'Or is it strictly on a need-to-know basis?'

'It's being given by the boss of Torchbearer Insurance, a major client of ours,' he said after a pause.

'And is your agency doing a good job for them?'

'The best,' he nodded.

'Then you should be among friends,' she said. 'So why trail a strange girl along with you?'

His mouth twisted. 'Call it—a different kind of insurance,' he said. 'Personal liability. And perhaps I should ask you a few questions before we get there—for a start, how old are you?'

'Twenty.' Telling him straight seemed better than some coy evasion.

'You look younger.'

So the carefully applied make-up hadn't supplied one atom of sophistication after all, she thought, and stifled a sigh.

'And what do you do for a living—when you're in work?'

'I'm a secretary,' she said. 'I do agency work here in the UK and Europe. I'm good with computers, and I speak French and a smattering of Italian. I also book restaurant tables, make excuses on behalf of my employer, send flowers, organise travel and collect dry-cleaning.'

'My God,' he said. 'You sound like a wife.'

She played with the chain on her bag. 'Doesn't Lynne do all that for you?'

'Yes,' he said. 'But she's actually going to be a wife, probably thanks to my specialised training.'

Somehow the outraged gasp she'd intended turned into a giggle. 'I wouldn't let her hear you say that.'

'Neither would I,' he said, and grinned back at her. 'So, what happened to the job? Was the restaurant overbooked? Did the flowers fail to arrive?'

Her throat tightened; she didn't look at him. 'There was a—misunderstanding which couldn't be resolved.'

There was a pause, then he said drily, 'I see.'

No, she thought, you don't. But it's still too new, too raw for me to talk about. And, even if the memory is still capable of making me feel sick to my stomach, you are the last person in the world I could ever confide in anyway.

She hurried into speech. 'Maybe you should tell me how I'm supposed to address you this evening. I can hardly go on saying—"Mr Radley-Smith."' She hesitated. 'Do I call you Rad, as Lynne does?'

'That's for working hours,' he said. 'In my more private moments, I prefer Jake. So make it that, please.'

She bit her lip, thinking the last thing she wanted was to be part of any of his private moments. She said tautly, 'I'll—try to remember.'

And when all this is over, she thought, I'll try even harder to forget.

The party was being held at the Arundel Club, just off Pall Mall. The entrance hall was like a grand foreign church, complete with classical statues, and Marin, self-conscious about the clatter of her heels on the wide marble staircase, wondered if she ought to tiptoe instead.

At the top of the stairs, they turned left into a wide corridor carpeted in dark blue. There were alcoves at intervals along the entire length, some with a small, gilded table displaying either a large and elaborate piece of antique ceramic or a flower arrangement, while others were occupied by small armchairs upholstered in gold-and-ivory stripes.

Jake Radley-Smith indicated a door on the right-hand side. 'The women's cloakroom,' he said laconically. 'You might want to check your wrap.'

'Yes,' she said. 'Thank you. I probably should.'

As she stepped inside, Marin was engulfed in a high-pitched chatter, and a clash of expensive perfumes. Handing over her shawl, she was aware of two girls next to her glancing at it, and then looking at her, before exchanging faintly derisive smiles.

No, she told herself. They're quite right. I don't belong here. I'll just have to keep thinking of the money and that will get me through.

She fussed with her hair for a minute or two and applied a touch more lipstick, waiting for the crowd to clear.

When she emerged into the corridor, Jake Radley-Smith was standing a few yards away, frowning at a large, predominantly brown landscape occupying the wall between two alcoves.

She made herself walk towards him and forced a smile. 'I'm ready.'

'Somehow,' he said, 'I rather doubt that.' As she reached him, he took her by the shoulders, spun her into the nearest alcove and kissed her very slowly, and extremely thoroughly, that astonishing mouth moving on hers with an expertise that turned her legs to water, and almost—*almost*—had her clinging to his shoulders to steady herself.

'What the *hell*,' she said furiously when she could speak, 'was all that in aid of?'

'Window dressing,' he told her calmly. 'Nothing to get uptight about. But I'm not usually seen with

anyone who looks quite so untouched, and people
might wonder.'

'You,' she said, her voice shaking, 'don't have to
be seen with me at all. This was your idea. Not mine.'

He said, 'Then consider the kiss an afterthought.'
He smiled at her. 'And it's worked. You look just
ruffled enough for people to wonder.'

Then he took her hand and walked her briskly to
the end of the corridor, where a pair of double doors
stood ajar, and ushered her into the room beyond
before she could think of a crushing remark—or
anything to say at all, for that matter. Because *ruffled*
was hardly the word to describe the welter of
emotion churning inside her.

The President's Room was vast, ornate, brightly
lit and full of people, all of them talking above the
efforts of a string quartet to play Mozart.

Almost as soon as they got inside, a male voice
called, 'Rad—good to see you. I've been wanting a
word.'

For a moment, they were surrounded, then
suddenly her companion was gone, drawn forward
on a wave of greetings into a group of other men and
hidden behind a wall of suits.

Which meant, thankfully, that she now had her
hand back, so all she needed to do was try to recover
her breath, along with some much-needed composure. And *not* touch a finger to her tingling mouth
to see if it was really as swollen as it felt.

Mr Radley-Smith was clearly someone who

intended even the least of his kisses to be remembered, she thought, swallowing. And his casual riposte of 'window dressing' was also going to linger in her mind for some time to come. As would 'afterthought'.

More than time for Operation Camouflage, she decided, unclenching her fists in order to take a glass of fresh orange juice from a proffered tray and looking round for sanctuary.

The crowd seemed to be drifting in the direction of the long buffet tables, where chefs in tall, white hats were waiting to carve from an enormous turkey as well as joints of beef and ham, for a moment, Marin's stomach lurched in longing. But she resisted temptation, telling herself she could still cook the pasta supper she'd originally planned when she got home.

She headed instead for one of the long windows which had been left open to the warm evening air, stepping out on to a tiny balcony with a wrought iron balustrade.

With a bit of luck, Mr Radley-Smith might think she'd taken advantage of his momentary inattention to disappear completely, she told herself, relishing the coolness of the orange juice against her dry throat.

But escaping from him out here was not proving as successful as she'd hoped. Instead, Marin found she was reviewing everything Lynne had ever said about him.

She knew for instance that, even without the company, he was a millionaire in his own right with a place in the country as well as a flat in Chelsea.

'Is he married?' she'd once asked, and Lynne had laughed.

'No, my pet, nor ever likely to be. Rad seems to have a sixth sense that warns him whenever the lady of the moment starts hearing wedding bells and—bingo—suddenly he's not really around any more. It's invariably done with a great deal of charm, but it's still over.

'And, of course, he spends quite a lot of time abroad, which helps.'

Before Marin had gone to work for the Ingram Organisation, Lynne had offered to see if there was anything suitable going at the agency.

'You might find it more interesting than being a glorified temp,' she'd urged, but Marin had shaken her head with determination.

'No,' she'd said. 'It's not for me.'

So, perhaps I have a sixth sense too, she thought as she finished her orange juice. Although it had seemed to go on the blink outside in the corridor, just now, or she'd have dodged.

Her haven was suddenly not as warm as it had been, either. A slight breeze had got up since sunset, and with a faint shiver she turned to go back inside.

Only to find her path firmly blocked.

The tall woman confronting her might be wearing the ubiquitous black, but her dress screamed French design, its severe lines relieved by the virtual collar of diamonds round her creamy throat. In her late twenties, she was reed-slim, like most of the other females in the room, and her blond hair was swept up into the kind of careless style that takes hours to achieve.

She was beautiful, with green eyes under impossibly long, mascaraed lashes, but there was no warmth in the glance surveying Marin.

And her tone was equally cold. 'Excuse me, but do you mind telling me who you are? I wasn't aware you were on our guest list for the evening.'

'She's with me, Diana,' Jake said easily as he appeared out of nowhere, walking to Marin's side and sliding an arm round her waist to draw her closer against him. 'Her name's Marin Wade. Darling, this is our hostess, Mrs Halsay.'

'I should have known, of course.' Mrs Halsay gave a musical laugh. 'Jake's invitations always say "and partner." His social life changes so rapidly, it's safer that way. So do forgive my lack of recognition.' She favoured Marin with a smile as radiant as it was brief, then turned back to Jake. 'Tell me, my sweet, where did you find this charming child?'

Jake shrugged. 'Let's just say that we found each other.'

Diana Halsay pouted at him. 'But how wicked of you to let her wander off alone, with so many potential predators hovering.'

'Don't concern yourself on that score,' Jake

drawled. 'Our separation was purely temporary, and I was extremely careful not to lose sight of her.'

'Well,' she said, sending another smiling glance in Marin's direction accompanied by the merest flicker of an eyebrow, 'If you neglect her again, I'm sure she'll find some delicious way to punish you. Now, take her off and feed her, my darling, and make sure you introduce her to all the people who are dying to meet her.'

For a moment, a slim hand burdened by a platinum wedding-ring and a diamond cluster as spectacular as her necklace rested on his sleeve, then she was gone.

'"Charming child,"' Marin repeated woodenly. 'Not a description ever applied to her, I'll bet.'

Jake's mouth twisted. 'In thirty years' time, sweetheart, you'll remember her words with a sigh of nostalgia. And, as hunger seems to be making you peevish, come and eat.'

Marin hung back. 'I'd prefer to do that at home.'

His brows lifted mockingly. 'Cocoa and a sandwich?'

She lifted a defiant chin. 'What's wrong with that?'

'Where would you like me to begin?' he murmured. 'Besides, your evening's work isn't over yet, so you need to keep your strength up.'

Led over to the buffet and made to choose, Marin found herself with a plateful of poached salmon, lobster mayonnaise and shrimp vol-au-vents, accompanied by a selection of exotic salads. And, in spite of her protests, a glass of champagne.

'One of humanity's greatest inventions,' Jake said, watching with faint amusement as she took a cautious sip. 'A wine that can be drunk at any hour of the day—or night.'

She said stonily, 'I'll just have to take your word for that, Mr Radley-Smith,' and went on with her supper.

When that was finished, she—met people. It would have been hard not to do so, she reflected, as her companion seemed to know everyone in the room. And all of them, apparently, wanted to know her too.

With Jake's arm draped casually round her shoulders, her tongue should have been glued to the roof of her mouth, but she actually found herself responding to the friendly overtures coming her way, and making shy conversation instead of feeling as awkward and self-conscious, as she usually did in these situations. She could even withstand the speculative glances from some of the other girls.

My ten minutes of fame, she thought ironically, as Jake Radley-Smith's latest squeeze. If only they knew!

One of the last people to approach them was the Torchbearer Insurance chairman, Graham Halsay. He was a tall man, slightly overweight, handsome with a florid complexion.

'Ah—Rad. Good to see you. Yes, very good.' There was a kind of awkward joviality in his voice. 'I feel we need to get together over the campaign for Torchbearer's new household policies, but my diary is full for the whole of next week.' He paused.

'However Diana has invited some people down to Queens Barton at the weekend, and I wondered—hoped that you might join us too.

'The pair of us could hammer out a few things in private, which would also give us a get-out from my wife's interminable sporting-contests.'

He gave a quick bray of laughter, then looked at Marin. 'And of course Diana absolutely insists that you bring your Miss—er—Wade with you. She found her quite delightful.'

Marin tensed, and felt the warning pressure of Jake's hand on hers.

He said, smiling, 'Thank you, Graham. We'd both be delighted. I'd love Marin to see the house, and the gardens must be looking fabulous.'

'Well, that's splendid,' Graham Halsay said a mite too heartily. 'First class, in fact. Really look forward to seeing you next Friday evening—both of you.'

Marin stood in silence, watching him go. When he was out of earshot, she said huskily, 'So what excuse do I invent—summer flu or food poisoning? If I blame the lobster mayonnaise, he may feel too guilty to ask any questions.'

Jake's mouth was set in a hard line. He said brusquely, 'No excuse will be necessary. I accepted the invitation on behalf of us both, and we will be spending next weekend at Queens Barton together. Let that be clearly understood.'

'No way.' Marin, startled, tried to pull her hand free and failed.

Jake leaned forward, his mouth smiling as he trailed a fingertip down the curve of her cheek, his eyes like chips of ice. His lips brushing her ear, he whispered, 'This is not up for public discussion, sweetheart. So save the argument until we're alone.' He paused. 'Now, smile back at me as if you have nothing on your mind but bedtime.'

And just how, exactly, do you do that? Marin wondered, producing a dutiful grimace and hoping it would pass. Especially when your bedtimes generally involved pyjamas and a good book.

Seething, she collected her wrap and walked downstairs with him in silence, climbed into the back of the taxi and huddled herself into the opposite corner to him while she tried to marshal her thoughts.

'So,' he said at last. 'What's the problem?'

She touched the tip of her tongue to her dry lips. 'I—I don't want to be involved in this. Not again. Not after this evening.'

Her voice shook. 'I may look younger than my age, and be called a child by the Queen of Diamonds back there, but that doesn't make me an idiot. And you were using me tonight as a decoy to fool her husband, because you're involved with—her. With Mrs Halsay. There's never an excuse for breaking up a marriage. So, never again, thank you.'

'Is that the case for the prosecution?' he asked, and there was a note of amusement in his voice which scraped along her nerve-endings.

She said stormily, 'It's all a joke to you, isn't it?
A game with peoples' lives—peoples' hearts. You
don't care that there are innocent parties in all this
who are going to be hurt.'

'Actually, I do care,' he said. 'Quite a lot. Particularly when the innocent party is myself.'

She gasped. 'You're pretending that you're not
having an affair with Mrs Halsay?'

'I'm pretending nothing,' he said calmly. 'Yes,
Diana and I were lovers for a time, but that was
eighteen months ago, while she was still Diana
Marriot. Only she was looking for a rich husband,
and I wasn't interested in marriage, as I made quite
clear from the first. She assumed she could make me
change my mind; I knew she wouldn't. She thought
if she issued an ultimatum and walked out, I'd come
after her. She was wrong about that too.'

*It's done with a great deal of charm, but it's still
over.* Lynne's words, thought Marin. And clearly no
idle comment.

'But she was the reason I was with you tonight,'
she flung back at him. 'You can't deny that.'

'I won't even try,' he drawled. 'You see, when
Diana finally realised that I'd meant what I said, she
looked around for a replacement and found Graham,
who was just getting over a nasty divorce and wanted
to prove it to the world with a glamorous new wife.
Naturally, I wasn't asked to the wedding, but after a
couple of months she wangled an invitation to a reception she knew I'd be attending.

'She was perfectly frank with me. Said she'd only married Graham because I wasn't available, but now could quite understand why his first wife had ditched him for someone younger and more fun in bed. And, on those very grounds, she suggested that our former relationship should be quickly and quietly resumed.

'She added that we'd need to be ultra-discreet, because Graham, due to his past problems, had a jealous streak, and regarded any of her previous involvements with suspicion.

'However, when I said a blunt and unequivocal "no" to her flattering invitation, she first of all didn't believe me. Insisted that she knew I still wanted her.'

Marin's throat tightened. 'And did you?'

'You've seen her,' he said laconically. 'And I've never professed to be made of stone. On the other hand, I've always known she could be big trouble. And her offer simply confirmed that.

'So I stayed politely adamant, and she got angry. Said that no one turned her down a second time, and that she was going to make me sorry for the way I'd treated her.

'That it would be quite easy for her to make Graham think that I was sniffing round her again, trying to restart our affair, and how would I like to see the Torchbearer Insurance account go up in smoke, as it were, as a consequence.'

He paused. 'However, she also suggested that under the circumstances I might like to rethink the whole situation, and fast. See sense, as she put it, and remember how good we'd been together.'

He added, 'Since then I've taken damned good care to be accompanied by a female companion at any events where she's also a guest. And, although it hasn't the slightest appeal for either of us, sweetheart, that's why you'll be accompanying me to Queens Barton next weekend.'

He took out his wallet as the cab drew up at its destination. 'We'll discuss the details over a nightcap. I presume you know how the coffee machine works?'

'You're—coming up with me?' She couldn't keep the dismay out of her voice. 'That won't be necessary.'

'I think it probably will,' he said. 'Unless you remembered to put Lynne's key in your bag before you left. No? I thought not.'

A mistake, she thought as she accompanied him mutinously up to the flat and waited resentfully for him to unlock the door, that she would try not to make again—like so many others.

'I'm going to have a brandy with my coffee,' he told her when they were back inside. 'May I get you one?'

'No,' she said. 'Thank you.'

'And I like my coffee filtered, black and without sugar,' he continued. 'As the world now believes we have breakfast together on a regular basis, that's something you'll be expected to know, and need to remember.'

'Then the world must be blind as well as stupid,' Marin said curtly. *Do you imagine any man would want a skinny, ugly little bitch like you?* For a moment, her memory blazed with the pain of those words.

She forced herself to add calmly, 'As for your ex-girlfriend, I'd bet good money that she wasn't fooled for a moment.'

'Then we'll have to be rather more convincing next time.'

'There isn't going to be any next time.' She glared at him. 'There can't. I'm sorry Mrs Halsay apparently finds you so irresistible, but this ludicrous bargain of ours was strictly a one-off. You had no right to accept an invitation to this house party without consulting me first. For all you know, I might have my own plans for next weekend.'

'Forgive me,' he said, the blue eyes merciless. 'But as you gave me the impression that you had nowhere to live and very little money, it never occurred to me that your social diary would be bursting at the seams.'

'It isn't,' she said. 'But that doesn't mean I'm willing to spend two days out of my life pretending we're in a relationship in order to keep your ex-mistress at bay.'

He said, on a note of polite enquiry, 'And presumably you also wish to forego the two thousand pounds I'm prepared to pay you to do exactly that?'

When Marin could speak, she said, 'You must be crazy.'

'No,' he said. 'Merely totally determined.'

'But your girlfriend will be over her virus by the weekend,' she protested. 'Surely you should be taking her?'

'Not,' he said, 'when the invitation was quite definitely extended to you.'

He paused. 'Now, I suggest you make that coffee, and when you come back we'll talk about what's really on your mind.'

He added softly, 'Which of course will be the sleeping arrangements.' And he smiled at her.

CHAPTER THREE

MARIN HAD LEARNED to make coffee in all kinds of ways, for all kinds of people, using all kinds of equipment, so once in the kitchen she was able to switch easily to auto-pilot and begin her preparations without scaldings or spillages, however much she might be shaking inside. As she undoubtedly was.

As the tantalising aroma of the rich, Colombian blend began to fill the air, she arranged white porcelain cups and saucers on a beech tray then leaned against the marble counter top, staring into space.

Something else to add to the dossier on the minus side, she thought without pleasure. Jake Radley-Smith had turned out to be a mind reader.

But then it didn't take too much perception to recognise all the implications of a weekend house-party in the country. Not when they'd been invited, and would presumably be treated as a couple.

He must have known that, she thought wildly, when he accepted the invitation. I suppose he imagined two thousand pounds would buy my compliance, but he's wrong.

And if the prospect of being left to Diana Halsay's tender mercies during the day while Jake was shut up with his host talking business chilled Marin's blood, the thought that she'd almost certainly be expected to spend her nights with him was infinitely worse.

I don't even want to contemplate that, she told herself. Or—my God—discuss it with him, either. I hoped he'd simply take no for an answer and opt for someone—anyone—else.

Because I'm not prepared to let myself be trapped into another situation that is none of my making, or made to appear as something I'm not. I—I can't. Not again.

But it was becoming painfully and worryingly obvious that, in addition to the rest of his flaws, Jake Radley-Smith was not someone who cared to have his wishes opposed.

Drawing a deep breath, Marin put the coffee jug on the tray and carried it into the living room.

Jake was occupying one of the sofas, coat and tie discarded and his waistcoat unfastened along with the top buttons on his shirt. A cut glass goblet containing his brandy was on the pale wooden table in front of him, and he looked casual, relaxed and—as if she needed any reminder—very much at home.

Whereas she felt as if she was treading over broken glass.

She put the tray down on the table next to the brandy, poured the coffee then sat down opposite him, feet together and hands folded in her lap.

'You look,' he said softly, 'as if you're about to be interviewed for a job, and if it makes you feel better, we'll play it that way. So let's move straight to pay and conditions. I'm offering two thousand pounds for you to continue to play the role of my girlfriend as you did tonight, but this time from mid-afternoon on Friday next to some point after lunch on Sunday. That's the deal on the table, and it won't change.'

She said bitterly, 'How simple you make it sound.'

'Because, unlike you, I'm not looking for complications,' he drawled.

'But it is complicated,' she said. 'It has to be. If we go there together, they'll think—that we are—together,' she finished lamely.

'In other words, we may end up sharing a bedroom and a bed.' He shrugged. 'You must have done so before. It's no big deal.'

He'd said earlier that night that she looked untouched, but presumably he believed that was only skin deep. That a girl of her age and generation was experienced enough to shrug off any potential awkwardness. Maybe even to find it amusing.

Only he couldn't be more wrong, she thought, swallowing down the bubble of hysteria threatening to rise in her throat. Yet she was reluctant to let him suspect her total innocence in case it amused him, although being laughed at might be the least of her worries.

'But in the past, it's always been my choice.' She

made herself speak steadily. 'That—might not be the case this time.'

'So, what's the matter, darling?' he asked, the blue eyes narrowing as he reached for his coffee. 'Scared I may not be able to spend two nights in your company without being overcome by lust?'

He shook his head. 'You really don't have to worry. I never make a serious move on a woman unless I receive a very definite invitation first. And I can't imagine anything of that kind coming my way from you. Right?'

Her face was burning. 'Absolutely right.'

'Said with true feeling,' he murmured. 'However, if it's any reassurance, in the past when I stayed at Queens Barton with a lady, admittedly in pre-Diana days, we were always given adjoining rooms. Mrs Martin, the housekeeper, is the old-fashioned kind.'

He paused. 'Naturally, I never bothered at the time to check if the communicating door locked, but I'm sure there'll be a chair you can wedge under the handle if you're worried I might sleepwalk.

'In fact,' he added, musing. 'I might even take the same precaution myself, in case your dreams send you wandering in the small hours.'

'They don't,' Marin said curtly. 'And I won't.' She picked up her own coffee. Drank. Braced herself. 'But there's also the question of "window dressing," as you call it,' she added, her blush deepening. 'I— I'd want that kept to a minimum.'

'Agreed,' he said promptly. 'Even a peck on the

cheek, arranged in advance and signed for in triplicate.'

She sent him a bitter look. 'It really is just a game to you, isn't it?'

'No,' he said with sudden harshness. 'It bloody well isn't. I am deadly serious about keeping Graham and Torchbearer on side, even if it means negotiating my way through a fairly tricky forty-eight hours, and the rest.'

His smile did not reach his eyes. 'And the great advantage of having you beside me, instead of some more accommodating companion, Miss Wade, is that, as I told you before, you're a total unknown.

'You said just now that you hadn't fooled Diana. Yet why else did she come flying over to accuse you of gate-crashing? Because you were a complete stranger, and it threw her. So she tried to find out who you were and what you were. And she's still no wiser, so you need to be prepared to answer some questions at your next encounter.'

'And what,' she said, 'am I supposed to tell her?'

He shrugged. 'As much or as little as you wish—apart from the fact that you're only with me because you're being paid.' He added thoughtfully, 'Tonight's air of shy mystery went down pretty well with most people.'

'Perhaps because it was perfectly genuine,' Marin said huskily. 'I am shy, and the real mystery was, what the hell was I doing getting mixed up with someone like you?' She shook her head. 'I think that things would have been a great deal easier if you'd just—married her as she wanted.'

'Not easier in any way that appeals to me,' he said drily. 'Besides, Miss Wade, I'm not the marrying kind. Has Lynne never mentioned that?'

She said too quickly, 'She doesn't talk about you.'

'What a paragon.' His tone was ironic. 'I must raise her salary.' He finished the rest of his brandy. 'So, what about it, sweetheart? What's your final answer? I'm offering honest pay for a couple of days of dishonest work, and you can't pretend you don't need the money.'

It galled her to acknowledge inwardly that he was right. 'I'm going to have you fired, you treacherous little slut,' had been Adela Mason's parting threat; if she succeeded, Marin would be in real trouble. The Ingram Organisation was built on trust; it had to be, when its staff spent so much time travelling with clients or staying in their homes. If Wendy Ingram believed she'd betrayed that trust so deeply and fundamentally, then Marin would be out in the cold with heaven only knew what kind of a reference.

And the search for another job could be long and arduous.

So could she really afford to turn down this offer, however loaded? And knew what her answer must be.

She gave a small, defeated sigh. 'Yes,' she muttered unwillingly. 'We have a deal.'

'Good.' He got to his feet. 'I'll be in touch during the week about the final arrangements. But before I go…' Reaching for his jacket, he took a cheque book and pen from an inside pocket. He wrote swiftly, signed his name and handed the cheque to her.

'For services already rendered,' he said.

She looked down at it. She said numbly, 'Five hundred pounds?'

'Isn't that enough?'

'More than enough.' She made a helpless gesture. 'All I did was stand there.'

'But you did it very decoratively,' he said. 'No one in the room would have dreamed it was just a business transaction.' He smiled at her. 'At times, I found it hard to remember that myself.'

So, Marin thought with sudden breathlessness, had she. Just once, and only for a moment when standing in the curve of his arm, she'd found herself fighting the temptation to lean back and rest her head against the strength of his shoulder. A brief battle he was totally unaware of and which, thankfully, she'd won.

And something she could not allow to happen again.

He shrugged on his coat and walked to the door. 'Until next weekend,' he said. His faint smile seemed to graze her skin. 'Goodnight, Miss Wade.' And went.

Leaving her staring after him, his cheque still clutched in her hand.

'So,' Lynne said, smiling, 'You've heard all about my weekend. How did yours go? I'm sorry I had to leave you in the lurch, honey, but if you had to be miserable at least it was in comfort.'

She gave Marin a long look. 'But you don't seem to have found your surroundings particularly restful,' she added candidly. 'On the contrary, you look as if you've barely slept. Are you still brooding over the sudden demise of the dream job?'

Marin bit her lip. 'And its possible repercussions,' she admitted.

'Come and tell me all about it while I get supper.' Lynne got to her feet. 'Mike's mother, the lovely Denise, sent me back with one of her home-made chicken and mushroom pies.'

'Don't you want to keep it to share with Mike?' Marin asked as she trailed after her into the kitchen.

'Certainly not,' said Lynne. 'He didn't offer me any of the leftover joint of beef she gave him.' She handed Marin a pack of French beans, a colander and a knife. 'Sort these out while I peel some potatoes.'

They worked for a few minutes in silence, then Lynne said gently, 'I'm listening, my lamb, so start talking.'

Marin bent her head. 'At first everything was fine. The weather was glorious and the house was beautiful, right on the edge of the village, with its own swimming pool. She—Ms Mason—told me to call her Adela, and even though she set quite a pace with the work I could cope easily. I was in seventh heaven.'

'But then?' Lynne prompted gently when she paused.

'Then her husband arrived, blond, smooth and

younger than her. He'd been in Germany, apparently, discussing some kind of business deal. I got the impression it hadn't gone too well, because there was a bit of an atmosphere. I was glad to get away.

'I was in a small flat that she'd recently had converted from some outbuildings. As she said, privacy for both of us.

'We always had a break after lunch, so the following afternoon I'd just got back from a swim when he, Greg, turned up. Said he wanted to have a look at the place and make sure the builders had done their job properly.

'I didn't want to let him in, but I couldn't very well refuse. So he wandered round, peering at the window frames and examining all the kitchen and bathroom fittings.'

She flushed. 'And he went into my room, which was awful, because the clothes I'd taken off earlier were on the bed, including my underwear. And he looked at me and grinned, and made some remark about me being untidy but that he wouldn't report me to the boss—this time.'

'I see.' Lynne's tone was grim. 'And when did this charmer make his move? Right then and there?'

Marin finished the beans and pushed the colander to one side. 'No. But I could feel him watching me all the time. I never gave him the least encouragement—I swear it.'

She took a deep breath. 'Then, a few days ago, Adela announced after lunch that she was driving to the *supermarché.* I—I thought he'd gone with her, so I went for my usual swim.'

She shuddered. 'When I went back to the flat, he was waiting for me in the bedroom. He said "Alone at last," and called me "sweet pea". I told him to get out, but he pushed me down on to the bed and started trying to undo my bikini top and kiss me at the same time. I—I realised he'd unzipped his trousers.

'I was struggling and trying so hard to scream that, when it started, for one crazy moment I thought it was actually me. Then Greg let me go, and I saw Adela standing in the doorway with her mouth open, making these dreadful sounds.

'I can remember thinking, "Oh, poor thing. She'll never forgive him for this." Then he got up and fastened his trousers, and started accusing me. Said I'd asked him over because the shower wasn't working properly and started flirting with him, but he'd thought it was a joke until I undid his zip, and said, "She's shopping. We're safe". And pulled him down on to the bed.

'He said I'd been coming on to him from the day he arrived, that I'd asked him to guess the colour of my underwear and then shown him it was white with pink roses.

'He said, "For God's sake, Del, look at her. She's no bloody oil painting. Who the hell would want to start anything with such a pathetic little object?"

'He said he hadn't told her about it because he felt sorry for me. He just never believed I'd go this far.'

Lynne gasped. 'Didn't you tell her what really happened?' she demanded.

Marin closed her eyes. 'I tried, but she didn't want to know. He'd got his story in first, and she believed him.

'Meanwhile, Adela was calling me foul names—"skinny little tart" being the most repeatable—and at one point I thought she was going to hit me, but by then Greg seemed to be in control because he stopped her. Said I wasn't worth it, and she should just get rid of me.'

She lifted her chin. 'So that's exactly what she did. I had to pack and get out. I'd have been stuck down there in the middle of nowhere but for Cecile, the housekeeper, who brought me some supper and told me her nephew would take me to Toulouse in his lorry first thing next morning if I wanted. I gathered that I hadn't been Greg's only victim.

'At Toulouse, I got on a flight thanks to a no-show, and here I am,' she added, trying a smile which collapsed.

Lynne said quietly, 'Bastard! Complete and utter bastard! And let's hope La Mason's next book's a stinker.'

She was equally upbeat about Marin's future prospects over supper.

'Up to this point you've had clients singing your praises. And if the worst happens you can stay on here while you're job-hunting.' She paused. 'I'll have to clear it with Rad, of course, as it's his flat and he's letting me camp here as a favour. However, there shouldn't be a problem.'

Marin hastily swallowed some chicken and was about to say, 'Actually...'

But Lynne was going on, 'Of course, I won't be here myself for much longer. Mike and I are starting to look for a flat to buy next week.' Her sudden smile was rapt and tender. 'We're planning the wedding for next year, and you have to be bridesmaid.'

She paused, frowning a little. 'And I shall also have to find my successor and train her up.'

'You're going to leave the agency?'

'Not immediately. But a married assistant will never do for Rad. He requires total commitment, and my priority is going to be Mike.' She cut herself another sliver of pie. 'I know you weren't keen a couple of years back,' she added thoughtfully, 'But you might consider working for Rad yourself, if push comes to shove.'

Marin drew a deep breath, telling herself that she had to break the news at some point. 'Oddly enough,' she said, trying to sound casual, 'I'm doing precisely that—in a manner of speaking.'

There was a silence, then Lynne put down her knife and fork, her eyes narrowing. 'Explain,' she said. 'Speaking in a manner I can understand.'

Marin considered and rejected a number of openings, and was left with the unvarnished truth.

She said baldly, 'He's hired me to be his girl-friend.'

She saw Lynne's expression turn to horror and added hastily. 'Well, pretend to be, anyway. He needed someone to take to a party. His real girl-friend couldn't go, and you were away, so he picked me.'

'Then he can just unpick you again,' Lynne said grimly. 'And I shall tell him so. When is this party?'

Marin bit her lip. 'Last Friday.'

Lynne closed her eyes. 'Dear God.'

'No, it's all right,' Marin assured her. 'It was business. It was fine. Nothing happened.'

Give or take a kiss, she thought uncomfortably, the memory of his arm around me and the warmth of him near me.

'Fine?' Lynne echoed derisively. 'After what's just happened in France?' She snorted. 'I'd say it's out of the frying pan into a very hot fire. Oh God, I could murder Rad for this.'

'If you really want to kill someone,' Marin said, 'Try a woman called Diana Halsay.'

There was a silence, then Lynne said wearily, 'Oh, bloody hell. Just when you think it's safe to go back in the water…' She sighed. 'I thought she'd finally abandoned the chase where Rad was concerned.'

'She has, in a way.' Marin pushed away her empty plate. 'Now she's trying to convince her husband that Ja…' She swallowed. 'That Mr Radley-Smith is chasing her instead.'

'So that the agency loses the Torchbearer business,' Lynne said grimly. 'My word, she must want her revenge very badly.' She looked at Marin. 'And, of course, Friday was the Torchbearer reception. It's been in the diary for weeks. I should have remembered.'

She paused. 'But I assumed Jake would be taking Celia Forrest.'

'She was ill.'

'I don't doubt it.' Lynne pulled a face. 'A condition brought on, no doubt, by the realisation that her application for the post of Mrs Radley-Smith, like so many others, has not been successful. She added cynically, 'But she'll get over it. One of his girl-friends told me that falling for Jake was rather like catching a virus—except that it was much easier to recover from once you'd got out of bed.'

Marin's face warmed. She said, 'I can't imagine why any woman would want him. He's far too fond of his own way.'

Lynne gave her an old-fashioned look. 'Well, he managed to persuade you to go to his party,' she commented. 'Why didn't you say no, and go on saying it until he got the message?'

Marin had a sudden memory of blue eyes lazily scanning her half-naked body. A voice saying, "We could always stay here together instead."

She thought—Because the alternative would have been so very much worse.

Aloud, she said lamely, 'He said he'd pay me. Very generously.' She tried to smile. 'It seemed like an offer I couldn't refuse.'

'As long as it was the only one.' Lynne smiled back, but her eyes were serious. 'And forget I suggested working for him. Once was clearly enough.'

Marin moved restively. 'Except it won't be,' she said in a low voice. 'The Halsays have invited us to their house in the country next weekend, and this time he's paying me four times as much to go with him, to keep up the pretence.'

There was a silence, then Lynne said softly and succinctly, 'Over my dead body.' She took a deep breath. 'Marin, you can't afford to get involved with Jake, believe me. He's out of your league, just as he was always out of mine.'

She shook her head. 'When I first started working for him, I could have gone overboard so easily, and don't think I wasn't tempted, but I saw the danger just in time and pulled back. Because I didn't want to be one more notch on his bedpost, and you mustn't settle for that, either. You're worth so much more.'

'But it's not like that,' Marin protested. 'The whole thing is strictly business, I promise. Separate rooms, everything. It couldn't possibly be anything else. I mean, look at me,' she added, Adela Mason's strident insults echoing in her mind.

'I'm looking,' Lynne said flatly. 'And I see a sweet and conspicuously innocent girl. Who should not be spending even a moment, let alone two days and nights, with a major predator like Jake Radley-Smith.

'Separate rooms?' She shook her head again. 'I'd prefer you in a separate universe. Because you would not be dealing with a fumbling amateur like that idiot in France.' She paused. 'Sweetheart, if you're worried about money, then stop. I'll match whatever he's offering, and you can pay me back as and when you can afford it.'

'When you're saving for a deposit on a flat and a wedding?' Marin bit her lip. 'Lynne, it's lovely of you to think of it, but he—Mr Radley-Smith's already given me five hundred pounds and promised me another two thousand after the weekend.' She saw Lynne's eyes widen. 'If Mrs Ingram fires me, I shall need it. And you couldn't possibly spare that much.'

'No,' her stepsister admitted ruefully. 'Probably not.' She sighed. 'But I still don't like this—any of it.' Her eyes glinted wrathfully. 'And I shall have a few things to say to my esteemed boss tomorrow morning.'

'No—please.' Marin was aghast. 'I made the agreement with him, and I can handle it. There are— ground rules in place.'

She tried to speak more lightly. 'And, after France, my sense of self-preservation has improved a hundred per cent. So you really don't have to worry. Because I'm not a child any more.'

'That,' Lynne informed her drily, 'is exactly the problem.' And she got up to clear the table.

CHAPTER FOUR

MARIN FOUND IT difficult to sleep that night. She told herself it was because she was dreading the coming interview with Mrs Ingram, but in her heart she knew she was restless because she hadn't been completely honest with Lynne.

Or, for that matter, with herself.

She turned over, punching irritably at her pillow. In retrospect, she now realised she'd been silly to think that, whatever the reason for it, she could remain totally immune to Jake's company. Especially that kiss.

I just wasn't expecting it, she thought defensively. That's all. Besides, I was off-balance from the moment he walked and caught me in that damned towel. And he made sure I stayed that way.

But now that she knew his potential danger, she would be more on her guard.

Besides, it was a house party, she reminded herself defensively. There would be other people around, and, for at least some of the time, Jake and Graham Halsay would be off talking business, so they wouldn't be in each other's pockets.

As for the hours of darkness—well, she would just have to trust that the Halsays' housekeeper would allocate the usual rooms, giving her privacy if not total peace of mind.

But she couldn't allow herself to think like that. From here on in, it was going to be strictly business. Forty-eight hours, she told herself. That was all. And when it was over she would never have to see him again, unless it was as a guest at Lynne's wedding next year.

Just two days and two nights and he would be out of her life.

She awoke later than she'd planned the following morning, to find the flat empty and a note from Lynne on the kitchen counter. 'You looked as if you needed your rest, it ran. I took some croissants and a loaf out of the freezer earlier, and there's cereal in the cupboard. Also plenty of eggs. I'll be back around six.' And, heavily underlined, 'Try not to worry.'

Marin scrambled the eggs and ate them with grilled smoked bacon, followed by toast with cherry jam and some strong coffee.

Then, dressed in a neat grey skirt and white blouse topped by a navy jacket, she set off for the Ingram Organisation.

Tina, the office secretary, greeted her wide-eyed. 'The phone line between here and France was burning up on Friday,' she whispered, and nodded towards Wendy Ingram's office door. 'Go right in. She's waiting for you.'

Mrs Ingram was on the phone when Marin entered, nodding briskly and making notes on a pad in front of her. She gestured to Marin to take a seat then, her call over, she put down her pen and leaned back in her chair.

'That's quite a can of worms you seem to have opened,' she observed caustically. 'According to Ms Mason, you're a home-wrecker—a sex-mad wolf in sheep's clothing who abused her hospitality, her kindness and her trust.' Her eyes narrowed. 'So, any comment?'

Marin met her gaze steadily. 'I think the lady is blaming the wrong wolf,' she said quietly, and gave a succinct and unemotional account of what had happened. 'I think, when she decided to hire me, she assumed it would be safe,' she added. 'That I wouldn't be his type.'

Wendy Ingram gave a sharp, angry sigh. 'I suspected as much. In the heat of the moment, Ms Mason said rather more than she intended. And she is now blacklisted.' She clicked on her computer and looked at the screen. 'But it leaves me with a difficulty about you. I have nothing until next week at the earliest, and that would be another residential job, running the admin for a veterinary practice in Essex.

'Their office manager is the sister of one of the vets, but she's off to Australia for a month, and her local replacement has broken her right arm quite badly so this is something of an emergency.'

She paused. 'You'd need to spend a couple of days being shown the ropes, and you'd be using Ginny Watson's flat.

She sighed. 'I was sending Fiona, but it seems she doesn't want to be apart from her boyfriend for four weeks, and this is a busy set-up, hardly likely to want someone moping about the place. So, how does it sound to you?'

Like the answer to a prayer, thought Marin. For so many reasons.

Aloud, she said, smiling, 'You can safely tell Fiona she's off the hook.'

She had a rich Bolognese sauce bubbling on the stove when Lynne returned that evening, a pan of water heating for the pasta and garlic bread waiting to go in the oven.

Lynne scented the air appreciatively. 'I think I'll hire you myself.'

'Too late.' Marin informed her. 'I'm off to deepest Essex next week to work for some vets. Small animals a speciality, which would seem to cut out wolves.' She smiled. 'And, as I'm now working again, I don't need any more money from Mr Radley-Smith. So next weekend is hereby cancelled.'

'Ah,' Lynne said quietly, and paused.

Marin stopped stirring the sauce and looked

at her. 'What's the matter? I thought you'd be cheering.'

'I probably would,' Lynne said grimly. 'If I hadn't spent much of the day fielding phone calls from Diana Halsay.' She shook her head. 'She's not giving up without a struggle.' She gave Marin a long look. 'I think Rad's relying on you, babe. In fact, I know he is, because I have orders to take you shopping tomorrow.'

'The only thing I'll be shopping for is more jeans and some wellies.' Marin lifted her chin. 'Naomi worked for a vet in Norfolk a couple of months back, and she said she spent a lot of time tramping behind him over ploughed fields.'

Lynne sighed. 'Well, before you go on this agricultural spree, could you turn your attention to a couple of evening dresses and all that goes with them instead—no expense spared?' She added gently. 'You know I wouldn't ask you to do this unless I thought it was necessary. And if it's any reassurance,' she went on, brightening. 'I told Rad that he wasn't your type.'

Marin swung round from the stove, aghast. 'Reassurance?' She shuddered. 'I bet that went down like a lead balloon.'

Lynne grinned. 'Not a bit of it. He said he'd already worked that out for himself. Anyway, he was quiet for a moment, then promised me on all he held sacred that he'd look after you and that you weren't to worry about a thing.'

'All Jake Radley-Smith holds sacred?' Marin gave a hollow laugh. 'That must be one of the shortest lists in the universe.'

Lynne's eyes narrowed as she poured the pasta into the boiling water and added a dash of olive oil. 'Whoa there, missy. He may be allergic to marriage, but that's not a hanging offence.

'Last night you were assuring me there was nothing to worry about, that you could cope and only the cash mattered. Now he's suddenly turned into Bluebeard. What's changed?'

Marin shrugged defensively. 'Perhaps I realised that you were right and I was wrong.'

'But the money would still be handy,' Lynne reminded her. 'The rent you're getting on your flat only covers the mortgage payments. You've nothing put away for contingencies.'

She added slowly, 'Besides, during the time I've worked for him I've never known Rad break his word, and, as he's said you'll be safe with him, I'd be inclined to give him the benefit of the doubt. But the final decision is yours, of course.'

And what happens, Marin thought wryly, giving her sauce a final stir, when the person I really don't trust in all this is myself?

Twenty-four hours later, reluctantly committed, she found herself the wary possessor of what amounted to a new wardrobe.

'But I don't need all this stuff,' she protested to

Lynne as she was herded inexorably from one store to another. 'It's such a waste when I'll never use it again. And I already have underwear,' she added defiantly.

'And very pretty it is too,' Lynne said kindly. 'But you may not be unpacking your own bag, and your hostess, who is well aware of Jake's private tastes, may take an interest in what you've brought. So you have to remember that you're supposed to be his girlfriend, and that everything you wear needs to exude man-appeal.'

Marin pursed her lips. 'And how degrading is that?'

'That,' said Lynne, a little smile dancing on her lips, 'Might depend on how you allegedly feel about the man. So this weekend definitely calls for silk and a fair amount of lace.'

She added briskly, 'And don't scowl like that, my pet. You're not paying for any of it, and when Sunday night comes you can stuff the whole lot into a bin liner, if you feel like it.'

'Don't worry,' Marin said through gritted teeth. 'I plan to.'

She dug her heels in, however, over the purchase of a bikini, insisting instead on a simple black maillot, and Lynne did not argue the point.

Her only comfort in all this, Marin reflected vindictively as she put each tissue-wrapped garment in the soft tan leather case, was that Mr Radley-Smith would never get to see most of these expensive trifles. Although he might wince when the credit-card bill arrived.

She was glad of the diversion that her Essex visit provided. The practice was busy and efficient, and the demands of the job well within her capacity. Ginny Watson was pleasant and friendly, and the self-contained flat over the garage that Marin would occupy was comfortable as well as compact.

She was going to Australia to see her boyfriend, Ginny confided, another vet who'd recently relocated there.

'He wanted me to go with him,' she said. 'But it's a big change, and I wasn't sure. However, we miss each other terribly, so I'm off to see if I like it there too.'

'How wonderful,' Marin said, wondering rather wistfully what it would be like to be wanted and needed from half a world away. 'I hope it all goes really well.'

Ginny eyed Marin thoughtfully. 'You're all right about staying down here for a whole month? Your boyfriend won't mind?'

'That was Fiona,' Marin said. 'I'm—free as air.'

Or I will be, she thought, her throat tightening. Once this weekend is behind me.

As she waited for Jake to come for her on Friday afternoon, tension was coiled inside her like a spring.

Punctual to the minute, he stood in the doorway of the living room, smiling faintly. 'So you haven't run away after all?'

The charcoal trousers he was wearing emphasised his lean hips and long legs, and the pale grey-and-white checked shirt was open at the neck, its sleeves rolled back over his forearms, revealing what she suspected would be an all-over tan.

'Did you think I would?' she challenged, suddenly dry-mouthed and despising herself.

She hadn't wanted the clothes he'd bought for her but, as she endured his critical scrutiny, she knew that the deep-red sleeveless top gave warmth to her pale skin and looked good teamed with the plain cream knee-length skirt, while elegant cream sandals added at least an inch to her height, plus a much-needed boost to her confidence.

What she was wearing underneath would be her little secret.

Her hair, which Lynne had ordained should be trimmed slightly, was newly washed and shining, and she'd made careful use of cosmetics to bring a glow of colour to her mouth and darken her long lashes.

He shrugged. 'I wasn't sure.' Once again he made no comment on her appearance, but simply picked up her case. 'Just this bag?'

'It's a weekend,' she said. 'Not a lifetime.' *Words she'd been repeating to herself continuously over the past days.*

His mouth twisted. 'Although it may seem like a lifetime before it's over,' he commented brusquely. 'Shall we go?'

The car waiting downstairs was low, sleek and powerful with a dashboard like the controls of a nuclear reactor.

'Typical,' Marin muttered under her breath as she slid into the passenger seat and adjusted her skirt. Yet, at the same time, the smell of expensive leather made her draw a swift, appreciative breath, and the comfort of the cushions which supported her was like a caress.

She desperately wanted him to drive badly, to be an arrogant, selfish risk-taker with a bad temper. Needed it, so that she could focus all her churning, fragmented feelings about him and channel them once and for all into dislike.

But she was to be disappointed, because of course he was none of those things and, instead, she was unwillingly forced to admire the skilful and patient way he dealt with the heavy traffic leaving London for the weekend.

'Do you drive?' he asked at last, breaking the tautness of the silence between them.

'I have a licence,' Marin said stiltedly. 'So I can do so if my work requires it. But there isn't much opportunity when I'm in the city.'

'Do you want to take a turn driving this?'

She gasped. 'My God, no.' Adding, 'Thank you,' as a hurried afterthought.

'As you wish,' he returned casually. 'I simply thought you might enjoy it. That it would start the weekend on a pleasant note at least, whatever happens later.'

'Are you expecting trouble?'

'If I was anticipating a restful break with close

friends, I'd be travelling alone,' he said caustically. 'As it is, I don't know what to expect, and that makes me uneasy. Let's just say I'll be glad when it's over.'

'Not nearly as much as I will,' Marin retorted.

His brief smile held no humour. 'I can believe it. Try to keep that particular viewpoint under wraps, will you?'

Once they were free of the capital, an hour's steady driving brought them to their destination. Queens Barton was an attractive village, its houses clustering round a well-kept green.

The house, Georgian in style and built of mellow brick, was situated down a private road some three hundred yards past the church, and approached through a tall, pillared gateway. Jake parked the car alongside several others on the broad, gravelled sweep at the front and came round to open Marin's door.

He said quietly, 'It's going to be all right. I promised your very scary stepsister I'd look after you, and so I will. Now stop worrying.'

He drew her towards him and for a brief instant Marin felt his lips brush her forehead, her eyes and her startled, parted lips.

When he stood back, she stared up at him, telling herself it was unimportant. A gesture. Trying to laugh about it but failing, she said huskily, 'More window dressing?'

'No,' he said quietly. 'Sheer self-indulgence, actually.' He took her hand and walked her across the neatly raked gravel. 'And here's our host, waiting for us.'

Graham Halsay was standing at the open front door, smiling expansively. He said heartily, 'Good to see you here again, Jake. And welcome, Miss… er…?'

She said in a voice that she managed somehow to make calm and pleasant in spite of her inner turmoil, 'My name's Marin, Mr Halsay, and it's lovely to be here.' She looked around her. 'Everything smells so fresh and beautiful after London.'

He nodded, his glance approving. 'My sanctuary,' he said. 'That's how I've always regarded it. And how it always will be.'

He ushered them into a large entrance-hall, its floor tiled in black and white. 'Diana's conferring with the cook, I believe, but Mrs Martin will show you to your rooms.'

At the sound of the plural, Marin almost sagged with relief. Avoiding Jake's ironic glance, she followed the housekeeper's plump figure up the wide sweep of staircase and right along a galleried landing. At the far end, an archway gave access to another much briefer flight of stairs, leading to a short passage.

Mrs Martin paused at the first door they reached and threw it open.

'This is your room, Miss Wade, and I hope you'll find it comfortable. Mr Radley-Smith will be next door,' she added, and Marin wondered if she'd imagined the slight emphasis in the words. 'Shall I send someone to unpack for you both?'

'I think we can manage, can't we, darling?' Jake said smoothly, and was accorded a faintly repressive smile before the older woman departed.

'Welcome to Queens Barton,' he said when they were alone. He walked over to the communicating door and flung it wide. 'As promised, I'm in here. The bathroom is across the passage, and I fear we have to share it. But the towels are twice the size of those at the flat, if that's any consolation,' he added silkily. 'Also, the door has a bolt.'

To her annoyance, she felt her face warm. 'Thank you.' Her voice was curt. 'I think I'll unpack now.'

'In other words, will I kindly retire to my side of the fence line and stay there,' Jake supplied with faint amusement. 'You don't feel we should leave the door open and practise our conversational skills?'

'I'd prefer a little time and space to myself,' Marin countered. 'To get my head together.'

He shrugged. 'Then I'll see you later.'

Left alone, Marin walked across to the window and knelt on its chintz-cushioned seat, lifting her face to the warmth of the sun, wanting it to remove the chill of unease within her that would not go away in spite of his assurances.

Their rooms were at the back of the house, she discovered, overlooking a sweep of manicured lawn and offering a glimpse of a swimming pool, currently unoccupied.

Under different circumstances, it really could be the setting for a perfect weekend, she thought, smothering a sigh.

She glanced across at the communicating door, now securely shut. It was an old door, stoutly constructed, and the walls were correspondingly thick, so there was no sound from the other room, no movement, or cough to remind her of Jake's presence. Yet she was as conscious of him as if the barrier between them had been made from thin glass.

Aware of the beguiling touch of his lips so fleetingly against hers only a few moments ago.

Oh, calm down, she adjured herself impatiently. Think of something else. Like the new job. But instead she found herself musing about Ginny, in love, and maybe preparing to sacrifice everything dear and familiar for the sake of her man.

Her thoughts travelled seamlessly on to Lynne, her clear eyes dreaming as she planned her home and her marriage, safe and secure in the certainty of Mike's devotion.

Whereas I, she told herself, swallowing, have never been even marginally in love, although now I seem to be falling in lust. And I don't know how to deal with it.

She sighed, leaning her forehead against the warm windowpane.

I should have been like Lynne, she thought, who saw the danger and made a conscious decision to stay immune.

Only I didn't—or perhaps I couldn't, which is even worse.

So the very last thing I should be doing is spending this weekend pretending that he's my lover and that all I want is to be alone with him, doing all the things that lovers do.

About which I know so much, of course, she added with bitter self-mockery.

'Self-indulgence,' Jake had said when he'd kissed her just now. But she couldn't afford that kind of luxury. Not when she knew how easily and fatally that could turn into self-betrayal.

She sighed again and wriggled off the seat. You're tired, she told herself. You haven't slept properly one night for the whole of the past week, and maybe you should rest now, because you're going to need all your wits about for the next forty-eight hours.

She kicked off her shoes and folded the chintz bedcover back to the foot of the bed before stretching out on the blue quilt beneath it and closing her eyes, letting her mind drift.

She was right on the edge of sleep when suddenly the communicating door was thrown open and she propped herself on an elbow, dazed and startled, as Jake strode in barefoot and minus his shirt.

Before Marin could move or utter a protest, he was on the bed with her, his body pinning her to the mattress, his hand sliding under her top to bare her midriff as his mouth came down hard on hers.

Marin found herself lifting her hands to his

shoulders, feeling the strength of bone and muscle under her fingertips as her whole body clenched in response.

But at the same moment, in some corner of her reeling mind, she heard a brisk tap on her door followed immediately by the faint squeak of a hinge as it opened, and realised they were no longer alone.

'Well, well,' said Diana Halsay.

She stood, smiling, while Jake reluctantly rolled away from Marin, dropping a kiss on her exposed skin before sitting up, pushing his dishevelled hair back from his face.

'I came to welcome my newest guest and make sure she had everything she wanted,' she went on. 'But I see you've forestalled me, Jake, darling.

'I never realised before that you were into a little afternoon delight, but one lives and learns.

'So, all I can say is please accept my abject apologies for this unwarranted intrusion. I shall have to be more careful in future.'

She turned back to the door, adding over her shoulder, 'If you can tear yourselves apart for long enough, tea is being served on the lawn.'

The bedroom door closed softly behind her, leaving them alone.

Marin drew a deep, shaky breath. 'You knew she was due to arrive?'

'I was about to go into the bathroom when I heard her speaking to someone at the end of the passage,' Jake said, his mouth twisting. 'I guessed she'd be on her way. It seemed a wise move to let her find us very much together.'

Did it? thought Marin, trying to find somewhere to look that did not involve bare, tanned skin. Trying to forget the swift brush of his lips on her body, as well as her own grave error in touching him, holding him. As if—as if…

'So,' he went on after a pause, 'Are you up for tea on the lawn?' He reached down and smoothed a strand of hair back from her flushed face, his fingers lingering. 'Or do you have any alternative suggestion, perhaps?'

'No,' she said, too quickly, flurried by the openly teasing note in his voice. 'Oh, no.' She swallowed. 'Tea would be—nice.'

And infinitely safer than the kind of forbidden fruit he represented. Because it would be so terribly easy to put out a hand and touch his skin, or the dark, curling hair on his chest, or run a fingertip along his mouth. To feel once more the warm weight of him pressing her down into the mattress…

'Then we'll make a joint and virtuous appearance in the garden in about thirty minutes,' Jake said, lifting himself lithely off the bed. 'This house is a bit of a labyrinth, so I'll knock on the door when I've showered and changed.' The smile he sent her was casual, friendly. Unambiguous. 'After all, I wouldn't want you to get lost.'

'But it's too late for that,' she wanted to cry after him as he walked back into his own room. 'Because

I'm lost already, and frightened that I won't find my way back to the girl I used to be when all this is over.'

And knew that was something else she would have to keep hidden over this nightmare of a weekend—whatever the cost.

CHAPTER FIVE

TEA ON THE lawn had such a wonderfully cosy sound, thought Marin as she dressed for dinner that evening. It spoke of sunlight, cucumber sandwiches and daisies twinkling in the grass.

Whereas the reality hadn't been nearly as inviting.

As she'd descended the terrace steps at Jake's side, and looked across the immaculately shorn grass to the cluster of parasol-shaded wicker chairs where Diana presided over a table set with an opulent silver tea-service, she'd known an ignominious desire to turn and run.

'All right?' Jake had asked softly, his fingers tightening momentarily round hers, and she'd nodded jerkily.

There were three other couples: Sylvia Bannister, a smart brunette, with her husband, Robert, a tall, red-faced man with an emphatic way of speaking; Chaz and Fiona Stratton, who ran their own antiques business; and the Dawsons, who were clearly older than the others, and probably friends of Graham rather than his wife.

After Diana's fairly perfunctory introductions, Marin took the first empty chair she saw and sank into it.

Jake dropped to the grass beside her chair, leaning back and resting his arm casually across her knees, a gesture of possession that she realised would not be lost on anyone present, as he undoubtedly intended.

It was like a little war, she thought, with herself caught in the middle. Maybe it was time she definitely established just whose side she was on.

It was apparent, for instance, that he'd washed his hair while he was showering and it shone, thick and glossy in the sunlight, only inches from her hand, offering her an irresistible opportunity for an intimate gesture of her own.

He's paying me, she told herself. Maybe I should start earning my money.

She let her hand drift down almost casually, stroking her fingers through the dark, silky strands, breathing as she bent towards him the beguiling scent of warm, clean skin, soap and the faint citrus aroma of some expensive shampoo. Everything, she thought, that she would forever associate with him. And as she did so she could have sworn she felt him tense.

Her hand slipped down to touch the damp tendrils at the nape of his neck. She said very softly, 'You didn't dry your hair properly.'

'I was in a hurry.' He turned his head, his eyes

smiling lazily, intimately up into hers. 'Next time, I'll get you to do it for me.'

She wished she didn't blush so easily, but after all she'd started this, so she could hardly back down now. She said sedately, 'It will be my pleasure.'

His smile widened to a grin. 'Now that I can guarantee,' he murmured.

'Consuela.' Diana Halsay spoke imperiously to the hovering olive-skinned maid. 'Please attend to my guests.'

Within seconds, a small table was placed beside Marin's chair and she and Jake were being offered plates providing a choice of tiny sandwiches of smoked salmon, egg and cress and some delicious pâté, plus Earl Grey tea served with lemon.

In spite of her inward churnings, Marin had managed to eat her share and chat to Clare Dawson, who was plump, grey-haired and disposed to be friendly.

As the party on the lawn eventually broke up, Diana announced, 'Tonight's strictly caz, darlings. I've invited some locals tomorrow, so we'll save the formality for then.'

But Jake had made it clear as they went up to their rooms that he didn't believe her. 'Diana doesn't do casual,' he said flatly. 'Or not as any ordinary person understands it. She's probably trying to wrong-foot you, so I suggest you wear something from the evening gear Lynne made you buy.'

She bit her lip. 'As you wish,' she agreed colour-lessly.

It was on that very subject that she and Lynne had come close to falling out, she recalled.

She'd looked at herself with horror in the changing-room mirror as she tried on the first dress. 'No way. My God, the skirt's too short and the top hardly exists.'

'What would you prefer?' Lynne had queried acidly. 'A nun's habit? For heaven's sake, honey, I thought you'd accepted that you're dressing as Rad's girlfriend rather than yourself. So please believe that shade of green is perfect for your colouring, and the *bustier* style makes the most of everything else you've got.' She'd paused. 'So stop complaining and try this next.'

This had turned out to be the dress she'd be wearing tonight, hardly more than a silky slip in turquoise, with a deep cross-over bodice and narrow straps.

Her protest to Lynne that she wouldn't be able to wear a bra under this had fallen on deaf ears.

'All the better,' her stepsister had commented breezily on the way to the cash desk.

You're dressing for a part, Marin reminded herself now as she twisted her hair into a loose knot on top of her head and secured it with a silver clip studded with yet more turquoise. Her earrings were silver too, in a simple spiral design, and she'd kept her make-up light.

But she felt hideously self-conscious when she opened her bedroom door to Jake's brief knock and saw his eyes widen.

She said quickly, 'Is it too much? Only you did say…'

'You look amazing,' he told her quietly. 'The other women will be eating their hearts out.'

She could see as soon as they entered the drawing room that Jake's instinct had been quite right. The men, including himself, were in dark lounge suits, but all the women were wearing cocktail dresses, Diana's being a midnight blue spangled affair that plunged to a dangerous depth at front and back. And a fleeting look of chagrin crossed her face when she saw Marin and what she was wearing.

Robert Bannister came over, cocktail shaker in hand. His eyes lingered on the soft curves revealed by Marin's bodice. 'Well, Jake, you've always been a lucky bastard, I'll grant you that.' He held up the shaker. 'Can I tempt you both to a Halsay Hand Grenade?'

Jake smiled calmly. 'A kind thought, but absolutely not. Marin would like white wine and soda, and I'll have a gin and tonic.'

When they were left alone, he added softly, 'If you hate spritzers, you can feed yours to one of Diana's plants. God knows there are enough of them around this room.'

Graham Halsay bore down on them. 'Someone getting drinks for you both? Excellent.' He smiled expansively. 'Jake, you already know everyone, so

let me take your charming companion under my
wing and perform some proper introductions.'

And quite suddenly, it all became easier, and she
was almost able to relax.

'That's a Fenella Finch dress, isn't it?' said Clare
Dawson. She sighed. 'She's my daughter's favourite
designer, but no use to me, I'm afraid.'

Her husband Jeffrey, a large, grey-haired man who
reminded Marin of her stepfather, smiled at her affec-
tionately. 'Well, I think you always look lovely,
darling.'

That's how marriage should be, Marin reflected
wistfully, thinking of her mother, loved devotedly by
two good men. Because it wasn't about good looks,
money and large houses but finding someone who
was your other half to complete you, make you
whole and safe. Then—keeping them close, for ever.

And wondered if she would ever be that lucky.

Her slightly sombre mood wasn't improved when
she went into dinner, and found she'd been seated
next to Robert Bannister with Jake placed on the
opposite side of the table and much further down.

However, the food was lovely, and she easily
resisted all Mr Bannister's slightly patronising
efforts to flirt with her, so the meal, although far
lengthier than she'd bargained for, was also less of
an ordeal than she'd feared.

And most of the conversation was general, which
meant she was not obliged to contribute.

Eventually, inevitably, the talk turned to the weather.

'You seem to have struck lucky again, Diana,' Chaz Stratton remarked. 'Do you have a secret deal with the great weather-man in the sky?'

Diana Halsay joined the general ripple of amusement round the table. 'Oh, how I wish it were true. It's such a nightmare trying to plan anything in an English summer. I suppose that's why so many people are moving further afield, finding themselves second homes near the Med.'

She flashed a smile at her husband. 'I've been trying hard to wheedle Graham into doing the same, but he's being awfully stubborn.'

'We have a second home, darling,' Graham Halsay reminded her quietly. 'In fact, we're having dinner in it right at this moment.'

'Of course,' she said swiftly. 'But it's a rather different story when it's lashing with rain outside in sub-zero temperatures.' She ticked off on her fingers. 'Leila James has a place near Marbella, Gilly Webb is looking for a big country house in Italy and another friend of mine has been immersed in a renovation project in the South of France.'

Her laugh tinkled out. 'And here am I, praying for two fine days in a row.'

'You keep up the pressure, Diana,' said Robert Bannister. 'Graham will give in eventually.'

Will he? Marin wondered, noting the host's set expression. Somehow, I doubt it.

'What about you, Miss Wade?' All eyes swivelled to Marin as Diana spoke, smiling. 'I'm sure you must have hankered for your own special place in the sun.'

Which is why, she's implying, that I'm dating a millionaire, thought Marin.

But she smiled back with the utmost tranquillity. 'I'm very fortunate, Mrs Halsay. My parents have a home in Portugal, and I spend a lot of time with them there.'

Or I would, if I didn't have to work so hard and so long in order to make a living.

'Really?' Diana said brightly. 'How fascinating.' And she changed the subject—and her target.

It was much later, while coffee was being served and she was taking a surreptitious look at her watch, that Marin found herself unexpectedly under her hostess's spotlight again.

'Do you swim at all, Miss Wade?' Diana enquired sweetly from the foot of the table during a lull in the conversation. 'Because my little Saturday morning gala is becoming quite a tradition. I do hope you'll feel able to take part in it.'

Well, that explained the session with Lynne in the sports department, Marin thought drily. She debated whether to mention that she'd swum for her school, and in a junior county team, and decided to keep quiet.

'Thank you,' she responded calmly. 'I shall look forward to it.'

'Excellent.' Diana's smile wafted past her to Jake. 'And I can't wait to see if anyone can beat you, darling.'

'I'm afraid you'll be disappointed, my dear.' Graham's intervention was also smiling but brisk. 'Jake and I have business to discuss tomorrow, which makes us both non-starters. I thought you understood that.'

There was a pause, then Diana sighed prettily. 'Ah, well.' She spread her hands in a humorous gesture of resignation. 'This is what happens when you marry a workaholic. But I'm sure I don't need to remind any of the wives present of that.'

She looked back at Marin. 'Beware, Miss Wade, of becoming involved with a man who puts the job first.'

In fact, thought Marin, you're really saying—don't get involved with Jake. Full stop. And you're addressing your own interests rather than mine.

She said composedly, 'I'll certainly bear your advice in mind, Mrs Halsay—if I'm ever tempted.'

As they left the dining room, Jake was momentarily detained by his host, and Marin found herself claimed by Sylvia Bannister.

'You've turned out to be the surprise of the weekend.' Her tone was faintly supercilious. 'How did you and Jake Radley-Smith become such an item? Or is it indiscreet to ask?'

'Certainly not,' Marin returned. 'We met through my sister. She works for him.'

'Oh.' The other woman was clearly surprised. 'But you don't?'

'Heavens, no.' Marin produced a mock shudder. 'That would be terribly unwise. Don't they say never mix business with pleasure?'

'I've heard it mentioned.' Mrs Bannister paused. 'So how do you earn a crust, if I may ask?'

'I work for the Ingram Organisation,' Marin said coolly. 'We supply a whole range of secretarial services for companies and private individuals.'

'You must be good at your job. It certainly seems to pay very well.' Sylvia Bannister ran a narrow-eyed glance over the Fenella Finch dress. 'And when did you meet Jake?'

Marin shrugged. 'A while back.' She added nonchalantly, 'But I seem to have known him for ever.' And she realised with a little shiver of awareness that it was no more than the truth.

Mrs Bannister's eyes narrowed. 'Well,' she said. 'You've been his best-kept secret until now.' She glanced towards Diana Halsay who was standing alone by the fireplace. 'No wonder…' She checked herself fsuddenly. 'But that's not important.'

'No,' Marin said gently. 'It isn't.' She smiled politely and turned away, then after a brief hesitation walked over to Diana.

She said quietly, 'I hope you'll excuse me, Mrs Halsay, if I say goodnight. It's been rather a long day.' *Nor do I want any more sessions with the Spanish Inquisition.*

'And will probably be a much longer night.' Diana's mouth smiled brightly, but her eyes were like stone. 'Do make sure, my pet, that Jake allows you just a little rest. We don't want to drag you out of the deep end tomorrow.'

Marin felt embarrassed colour flood her face, but she kept her voice steady. 'Thanks for the advice, Mrs Halsay, but I think I'll manage to keep afloat.' She added lightly, 'Besides, Jake's not an easy man to refuse.'

I'll probably have to pay for that, she thought with a soundless sigh as she turned away. I hope it was worth it.

She was in her room, replacing her dress in the wardrobe, when there was a knock on the door and Jake's voice said, 'Marin—a word, please.'

She hesitated. 'Can't it wait until tomorrow? I—I'm rather tired.'

'I'd rather we spoke now.' He paused, then added flatly, 'I'll count to three, then I'm coming in.'

To find her, she realised numbly, naked except for a pair of lace briefs.

She heard him say, 'One…' and called back, her voice strangled, 'No, wait—please.'

Hastily she searched along the rail for the pretty ivory satin robe which Lynne had insisted should be added to their haul and dragged it from its hanger, thrusting her arms into its sleeves and knotting the sash firmly round her slender waist.

As she opened the door, Jake walked past her into the room and stood hands on hips, viewing her critically. 'I must remember to tell Lynne that her taste is faultless,' he commented.

She lifted her chin. 'If that's all you came to say, it could certainly have waited.'

'I don't do waiting,' he said. 'I thought you'd have picked up on that by now. But I wanted to talk about something else.' He paused. 'Clare Dawson, who's taken a shine to you, told me quietly that you seemed to be having a minor confrontation with Diana just now, and she was afraid you could have retired hurt.' He shook his head. 'I should have been with you to draw her fire.'

Marin bit her lip. 'No need.' She forced a smile. 'I think I actually came off best from the encounter—this time, at least.'

He said with a touch of harshness, 'And I fear she's just getting into her stride. Goddamn it, I should have said no to Graham's invitation and insisted on a weekday meeting instead.'

Marin shrugged. 'I've been in worse situations.' She thought of Greg and her skin felt suddenly clammy.

'Then you have my sympathy.' His mouth twisted wryly. 'However, you don't have to take part in Diana's swimming fest tomorrow, if you'd rather not. I can find some way of getting you out of it.'

'After you've bought me a new swimsuit?' Marin enquired coolly. 'I wouldn't dream of it. And I'll try not to make a complete fool of myself.'

'One more thing,' he said softly. 'Is there really a villa in Portugal?'

'Yes, of course. I wouldn't lie about a thing like that. Has Lynne never mentioned it?'

'Maybe,' he said. 'Even—probably. Although we don't share every facet of our lives.'

'For which she must be eternally grateful.' The thought translated itself into words and escaped aloud before she could stop herself.

His eyes narrowed. 'Save your claws for when they're needed,' he directed coolly. 'Don't sharpen them on me.' He paused. 'I asked about Portugal only because I'm surprised you didn't go there when the job went pear-shaped. Wouldn't your parents have helped you?'

'Yes,' Marin said. 'But I've always tried to remain independent. Manage alone, whatever happened.' And if I'd even hinted about Greg's behaviour, she thought, Derek would have gone looking for him with an axe.

'But instead you turned to Lynne and fell into my evil clutches.' His mouth twisted. 'Portugal might have been the safer option, my sweet.'

'Safer, but fraught with long-term difficulties, because they'd have wanted me to stay. Whereas in another thirty-six hours all this will be over, Mr Radley-Smith, and you and I will never have to meet again.'

She took a breath. 'And, now that's settled, I'm sure you'll want to rejoin your friends downstairs.'

His brows lifted. 'Not when you let it be known you were having an early night,' he observed caustically. 'That would be considered in most circles as a delicate hint to me to join you without delay.'

He added softly, 'Believe me, sweetheart, they won't be expecting to see either of us until we arrive exhausted but ecstatic at tomorrow's breakfast table.'

'Yes, that was what Mrs Halsay implied.' Her face was burning again. 'But I just wanted to get away. I—I wasn't thinking when I said it.'

'No?' He smiled at her. 'And I thought it was all part of some cunning plan.'

'I don't think I'm that devious,' Marin said ruefully.

'No,' Jake said slowly. 'I don't think so, either.' He walked over to her and stood looking down into her face, the blue eyes sombre as they searched hers. 'I should never have involved you in all this,' he said quietly. 'I don't often suffer from regrets, but this is one of those rare occasions.'

She was trembling inside, her voice husky as she said, 'Well, it's too late to turn back now.'

'Yes,' he said, and there was an odd almost bitter note in his voice. 'I know it is.' He framed her face in hands that felt as cool as water against her flushed skin and held her for a long moment. He said softly, 'Goodnight, Marin. Sleep well.'

He let his gaze rest on her parted lips, then after an almost palpable hesitation stepped back, turning in the direction of his own room.

Motionless, she watched him go, heard the click as the door closed behind him, lifted a hand to touch the mouth she'd thought he was about to kiss. Knowing how much she'd wanted him to do precisely that.

Wondering if he'd known too—had guessed somehow—and decided to let her down lightly with his refusal.

And, if that was indeed so, trying quite desperately to feel grateful.

She spent a restless night, her sleep interspersed with fitful dreams, and woke all too early in a bed that looked as if it had been hit by a cyclone. She then had to decide whether to get up and re-make it, or simply get up. And, feeling hot, sticky and frazzled, she went for the latter option.

She trod over to the window and knelt on the seat, resting her forehead against the coolness of the glass. Everything was still, the sky a hazy blue, the sun already gathering strength.

A walk in the garden, she thought. Peace and quiet to bolster her for the day ahead, and the storm clouds hovering not far away which had nothing to do with the weather.

She showered swiftly, then dressed with equal speed in a pair of white linen cropped trousers, and a dark blue sleeveless top, keeping one eye on the communicating door as if expecting it to open at any moment. Which was ridiculous, bordering on paranoid, when it was still as firmly closed as it had been when Jake had left her the previous night.

I have to start trusting him, she thought as she brushed her hair, then paused, wondering uneasily if it could possibly be herself she didn't trust as she remembered vague but embarrassing fragments of last night's dreams.

But she couldn't afford that kind of speculation.

She had to think of the money, and only of the money she reminded herself as she made her way downstairs. If she concentrated on that and nothing else, in another twenty-four hours all this would be over and her life would be back under her own exclusive control once again.

As she reached the ground floor, the chink of crockery from the dining room and a murmur of voices indicated that the staff were already busy preparing for breakfast. The drawing room was deserted, however, the French windows standing wide open to air the room, and she slipped out noiselessly on to the terrace and went down the broad steps.

The lawn was damp with early dew, and the air had a clarity and freshness not discernible in the house.

Marin knew where the pool was, because Clare Dawson had been talking regretfully before dinner last night about the herb garden that had been destroyed to make way for it by Graham's first wife. She followed the path down to a high brick wall and pushed open the wrought iron gate.

As she walked in, a bird rose from one of the climbing roses growing round the enclosing walls and flew away with a trill of warning, leaving only silence.

Whatever the charms of the herb garden might have been, Marin felt as she looked around her that the first Mrs Halsay had made a good job of the conversion. There was a wooden changing pavilion painted pale yellow at one end, while wrought iron tables with cushioned chairs and parasols in pastel colours that matched the roses were set in groups round the pool.

She stood for a long moment, eyes half-closed, breathing the scent of the flowers in the warm, still air. Then she moved across the flagstones to the side of the pool and knelt, dabbling an exploratory hand in the turquoise water.

'Trying to get some secret practice, Miss Wade?' Diana Halsay's voice made her start.

Mentally cursing the premature loss of her solitude, and its cause, Marin got to her feet and turned to face her hostess who was standing a couple of yards away, glossy in grey linen trousers and a matching silky top.

She said composedly, 'Just testing the waters, Mrs Halsay.'

'You're certainly an early riser,' Diana commented. 'Fresh as a rose too. You've really impressed my husband. He was saying last night that you were what the French call *"belle-laide"*. Not strictly a beauty, but with an odd kind of attraction just the same.'

'How very flattering.' Marin lifted her chin. 'I didn't know I warranted being a topic of conversation.'

Diana gave her an old-fashioned look. 'Oh, come on, sweetie. Not even you can be that naïve. But understand this. Whatever game you're playing with

Jake isn't fooling anyone, except perhaps poor old Graham, who thinks you're a really nice girl.'

Marin said tautly, 'I don't know what you're talking about. There is no game.'

'I hope not.' Diana's smile did not reach her eyes. 'Because I promise that you're in a strictly no-win situation.'

'Trying to undermine the opposition, Diana?' Jake asked from the gateway. 'Isn't that against the rules?' He walked over to Marin, put a hand under her chin and bent to kiss her lightly on the lips. 'You were missing when I woke up,' he said softly. 'That's not allowed, either.'

'One of the things we always had in common, darling,' said Diana. 'We both made our own rules and changed them whenever we wished. Maybe we should all remember that.' She added, 'Breakfast is being served—if either of you are interested.'

And, on that, she sauntered to the gate and disappeared, leaving them alone together.

CHAPTER SIX

JAKE'S HAND WAS still clasping Marin's chin as he looked down into her eyes.

He said quietly, 'Are you all right?'

'Of course.' She freed herself, stepping back. 'How did you know where I was?'

'I saw you from the bedroom, crossing the lawn. I wanted to talk to you anyway, but then I saw Diana following you and decided to hurry.'

She said stiltedly, 'She doesn't believe it. That we're involved—having an affair.'

'Did she say so?'

She looked past him. 'Pretty much.'

'Then we'll have to try to be more convincing.' He nodded at a wooden bench set against the wall. 'Shall we sit down?'

She hesitated. 'Shouldn't we go back for breakfast?'

'There's plenty of time. Besides, we do need to talk, and this seems relatively neutral territory.'

'Talk about what?' she asked as she reluctantly took a seat beside him.

He shrugged. 'Maybe explore the vast uncharted

wastes of all the things we still don't know about each other. I wouldn't want to be caught out again by something like the house in Portugal.'

'That's hardly likely.' She stared down at the flagstones. 'Besides, I think we know enough to get us through the next twenty-four hours.'

'After which?'

'After which we revert to being strangers,' Marin returned, ignoring the sudden thump of her heart. 'Getting on with our very separate lives,' she added with emphasis.

'Well, there we differ,' he said softly. 'Because I think the mutual learning-process has just begun. And that our lives are going to be far from separate.'

Her glance was wary. 'What do you mean?'

'You're currently occupying my property,' he reminded her, his voice silky. 'You must admit that creates a connection.'

'If so, it's a temporary one that I'm anxious to cut as soon as possible,' Marin said grittily. *Nor does it make me your property.* 'Now I still have a job, I can soon find alternative accommodation, and I shall.'

'Tell me something,' he said, after a pause. 'Are you this prickly with all your clients?'

'No,' she said. 'Anyway, you're not a client.'

'No?' Jake queried, the blue eyes scanning her speculatively. 'Even when, like them, I'm paying quite generously for your services, Miss Wade? So, how do you regard me, then?'

'You're Lynne's boss.' She swallowed. 'That's all. I—I don't need to know anything else.'

'If that's true,' he said slowly, 'Why do I get the distinct impression I've been tried and found wanting?'

Marin glanced away. 'Now you're being absurd.'

'I don't think so,' he returned. 'So what's the problem? I thought I'd made it clear you can trust me not to step out of line, except in dire emergency.'

She remembered the warm weight of his body pressing her down into the bed, the glide of his fingers uncovering, discovering her exposed flesh. And all for Diana, watching from the doorway with her fixed, unsmiling smile.

No, she thought. He didn't cross the line even then. I could have been a waxwork—or even one of those blow-up dolls.

'Maybe I feel that convincing you I'm reliable is a big step towards proving to Graham that he has nothing to fear from me, either.'

He added bleakly, 'And my need to do that has no connection with his being a client.'

She said, 'You really like Mr Halsay, don't you?'

'Yes,' he said. 'And I admire him too, apart from his unerring ability to pick the wrong women.'

She gasped. 'Are you saying your own choices have always been impeccable?'

'No.' Jake's tone held a touch of chill. 'But I don't marry my mistakes.'

Or at all, she thought. Which is why you'd rather

pretend to be close to me instead of raising the hopes of any of the girls you're seeing, like Celia Forrest. Because you know there's no danger of me taking you seriously—of being fooled by the way you seem to look at me sometimes, the warmth I think I hear in your voice.

Because I don't need to be reminded that I'm your paid employee, and compared to Diana Halsay, I don't even feature.

Yet you still can't resist trying to make me respond even marginally to your charm. Because it's all technique—the seducer's check-list, and as natural to you as breathing. Nothing else.

Which means that all the real resistance has to come from me, and fighting you mentally and emotionally, as I know I must, is becoming so difficult that it scares me. Makes me dread what could happen to me if I don't take care.

Aloud, she said tautly, 'But then, Mr Radley-Smith, you're not interested in marrying anyone. So maybe you should make allowances for lesser mortals.'

She rose to her feet. 'Now, unless you have anything further to discuss, I'm going back to the house. I need some food to build up my stamina for the swimathon.'

He stood too. 'I'm going to stay here for a while. I have some thinking to do.' He paused. 'I'm sorry I shan't be around to cheer you on, but this meeting with Graham is important.'

She said quietly, 'I know it is. And it's why I'm here. The only reason.'

'Not quite,' he said. 'You seem to be forgetting the money. And that would never do.' He sent her a brief, impersonal smile. 'I'll see you later.'

'Yes,' Marin said, and walked away from him. She didn't look back, even when she reached the gate and thought she heard him say her name.

It was scorchingly hot, and Marin was glad of the shade of the parasol as she waited tensely for the final race. The men had swum first and Chaz had eventually beaten Rob Bannister to emerge the winner.

When it was the turn of the women, Clare Dawson had declared firmly, like her husband, that she was no swimmer and would watch. In the first heat, Diana had an easy win over Fiona Stratton, and Marin had little trouble beating Sylvia Bannister, a good but showy swimmer, in the second.

But the real battle of the morning was about to take place, and everyone round the pool knew it—and also knew it had little to do with being the fastest swimmer.

Diana was powerful and sinuous in the water, rather like an anaconda, thought Marin. And the white bikini the older woman was wearing was frankly minimal, showing off her sexy figure to the limit.

By contrast, Marin was well aware that her simple black swimsuit would not win many prizes for its seductive qualities. And, judging by the smiles that Sylvia and Diana could not be bothered to hide, they totally agreed with her. But her suit's sleek, untrammelled lines were just what she needed in the water, her long hair pinned up into a neat knot.

Rob Bannister was loudly offering odds on Diana to win, and Fiona's husband, Chaz, was also backing his hostess.

'We're supporting you, dear,' Clare Dawson whispered to Marin. 'Don't let us down now.'

Marin slid into the water and waited for Diana to join her. Her eventual arrival was greeted with applause and shouted encouragement.

Then the signal was given and they were off, Diana powering her way recklessly through the water, and Marin's controlled, easy crawl keeping her just about on level terms. She'd known from the beginning that it would all depend on the turn, and so it proved. She touched the tiled surround at the far end then kicked off strongly, giving it everything she'd got, propelling herself into the lead while the other woman was still floundering.

She could hear Diana splashing and gasping beside her, trying to claw back the advantage, but she'd put too much effort into the first length and had little in reserve. Certainly not enough to catch Marin as she struck for home, coming in at least three seconds ahead.

She clung to the edge, eyes closed as she tried to recover her breath and not listen to the subdued commiserations and murmurs of, 'Bad luck,' greeting her opponent.

Then strong hands slid under her armpits, lifting her clear out of the water and setting her down on the tiles. She only realised the pressure she'd been under when she felt her legs shaking beneath her, threatening to collapse, and found herself being lifted bodily into a hard, male embrace.

'Sweetheart.' There was laughter in Jake's voice. 'I'm losing count of your hidden talents.' Holding her still off her feet against the lithe strength of his body, he kissed her, his lips parting hers in total mastery, total possession.

She found she was clinging to him in return, drenched as she was, her arms round his neck, her legs wrapped round his hips, and her startled, ravished mouth yielding every last breathless drop of its sweetness to the pagan, demanding invasion of his tongue.

Her senses were going crazy, responding to the warmth, to the taste of him. To the already familiar scent of his skin.

And she felt the sharp, insistent ache deep, deep inside her of a need she had never before had cause to recognise, let alone acknowledge.

Then, as the world seemed to be spinning deliriously into oblivion, Jake lifted his head, lowering her gently to the ground and holding her in firm hands until her breathing steadied and she could stand unaided.

She heard him whisper, 'My clever angel,' as he

kissed her again, this time, very gently, very tenderly, on the tip of her nose.

At that moment, too, Marin became aware of the silence. Realised with scalding embarrassment that this had been no intimate moment but public property. And quite deliberately staged.

Everyone was watching them: Jeff and Clare turning to exchange significant glances; Graham smiling in faintly whimsical approval; Sylvia Bannister with brows raised while her husband scowled; the Strattons frankly open-mouthed, as Chaz grasped his prize of a bottle of Cristal.

As Marin attempted to clutch at what was left of her composure, she saw Diana advancing on her, holding more champagne, her brilliant smile looking as if it had just been painted there.

'To the victor, the spoils!' she exclaimed brightly. She looked from Marin to Jake and back again, her glance darting like a snake's tongue.

'Although I suspect your real reward will come rather later,' she added with a little trill of laughter which made Marin long to slap her hard.

'Diana.' Graham's voice was quiet, but it found its mark. 'You're embarrassing Miss Wade.'

'Oh, surely not? She's a woman of the world, after all, and can stand a little teasing. All in all, she's quite a revelation—isn't she, Jake, darling?'

He looked back at her, his face cool and unsmiling. 'From the moment we met,' he drawled, 'She has never failed to take my breath away.'

The smile never wavered, but there was a flash of real chagrin in Diana's eyes.

If I thought for one minute she was truly in love with him, Marin reflected with curious detachment as she accepted the Cristal with a sedate word of thanks, I could almost feel sorry for her.

Because realising that you want the totally unattainable, and that no other man apart from him will ever fulfil you and make you happy, has to be the ultimate agony. Total heartbreak. The kind of nightmare from which you never wake.

Something which I dare not risk.

So why—*why*—did I kiss him back like that? Let him do what he did, as if it was no longer part of the pretence?

I think, she told herself dazedly, that I must be going mad.

Jake fetched her towel and wrapped it round her sarong-style. He said softly, 'Come on, darling. Let's get you showered and changed. It's nearly lunchtime.'

She heard herself murmur something that might have been assent in a small, wooden voice as she slid her feet into her sandals and handed him the champagne.

Her legs were still trembling as she walked beside him back to the house.

She said, 'You're soaking wet. Your clothes must be ruined.'

'They'll survive,' he said. 'And so shall I.'

'You mentioned the shower deliberately, didn't you?' she muttered. 'So that they'll think we're going to take one together. This is what you meant by being more convincing.'

'Of course,' he said curtly. 'What else did you expect?' He added, 'But, as we both know it isn't true, why should you care?'

'I—I don't.' Her response was swift, but not as definite as it should have been, and she knew it.

Knew also that he was far too experienced not to have gauged her reaction to his kiss. Even worse, he might even have been amused by it, and by the fact that he'd been the one to call a halt, she thought, dying inside.

He paused, the blue eyes travelling over her. 'By the way, I seem to recall specifying a bikini to Lynne, and not some one-piece effort. What happened?'

'I made a decision of my own,' Marin said, lifting her chin. 'Dressing for the part is one thing. Undressing is another.'

There was sudden amusement in his voice. 'I'll try to remember that.'

She searched hastily for a change of subject, something more impersonal. 'How—how did your meeting go?'

'It went well. Better than I could have hoped for a month ago.' He paused, his mouth twisting into a faint smile. 'And you've made a real hit with Graham. I suspect if he was your father he'd be asking my intentions.'

'And you, of course, would be telling him they were strictly dishonourable.' She managed somehow to infuse some lightness into her tone.

'And leaving before he could find the shotgun,' Jake agreed drily. 'However, as part of the improvement in our relationship Graham's asked me to play golf with him this afternoon. I said I'd check with you first—that you might like to go for a drive instead—see something of the countryside.'

'No, no,' Marin denied hurriedly. 'Golf is fine.'

'You could come too,' he suggested. 'Walk round with us.'

She remembered happy times doing exactly that with her stepfather, and for a moment was tempted. Then common sense reasserted itself, and she shook her head.

'We hardly want to give the impression we're joined at the hip,' she said. 'I don't think anyone would believe that, either.'

Jake shrugged. 'If you say so. But be warned, Diana has a croquet event planned after lunch. She'll want revenge for this morning's miscalculation.'

'Then she'll be disappointed,' Marin said crisply. 'For one thing, I wouldn't trust myself around her with a mallet in my hand.' She paused, then said with constraint, 'Besides, the swimming thing was horrid.'

'You deserved to win,' he said. 'You're bloody good.'

She said, 'But she fixed the draw, didn't she, so we'd be in the final together?'

'Almost certainly,' Jake agreed.

'So it was nothing to do with real swimming. But then nothing this weekend is what it seems.'

Least of all the way you kissed me, as if you were staking some claim, telling the world that I was yours, to be taken just as soon as we were alone...

'No,' Jake said abruptly. 'It isn't. But you must have known that's how it would be.' He gave a short sigh. 'However, it will be over soon, and then it's back to reality. Comfort yourself with that.'

Comfort, she thought, offering a small, taut smile, was hardly the word she'd have chosen.

As they reached her door, Jake made to hand over the Cristal, but Marin shook her head. 'No, you keep it—please.'

'Marin,' he said quietly, 'This is one of the truly great champagnes. You won it. It belongs to you.'

She turned away, reaching for the door handle. 'It's also very expensive. Even I know that. So it would be wasted on me, because it deserves a big occasion—a great reason to celebrate.' She looked back at him, smiled. 'And that's far more your life than mine.'

She added, 'A touch of the reality you mentioned.'

Then she went into her room and gently closed the door behind her.

Strange how time dragged when you were counting the hours, thought Marin, taking a reflective sip of her iced orange juice and bitter lemon.

Firstly, the hours until dinner. Then the hours until bedtime. Then the hours between breakfast and the blessed moment when Jake would drive them both back to London and it would all be over at last.

At which time her life would finally be able to resume some semblance of normality. Or so she hoped.

A new job to go to, she thought, and a chance to reassure Wendy Ingram that she was still to be totally relied upon. Plus—and maybe this was most important of all—a much-needed opportunity to get her head together and stop drifting off into the kind of forbidden fantasies she was ashamed to contemplate.

Jake had left for the golf club with Graham immediately after lunch, and she swiftly excused herself from the proposed croquet competition on the grounds that she wanted to go for a walk. No one, she noted with irony, had attempted to dissuade her.

She headed for the village, but most of it seemed to be shut—even the church—so she bought a drink in the village pub, discovered a shaded corner of its garden, found an unused page in her diary and began with a certain gritted determination to write down what she'd need to pack for Essex.

Planning for the future, she told herself, and letting the immediate present take care of itself. That was what she needed to do. And finding somewhere else to live when she returned from Essex was a matter of urgency.

Because she could not go on being Jake's tenant, even in the short term. She had to distance herself from him totally. Make sure she had no reason even to set eyes on him again until she could be sure he was out of her system for good.

She might even have a man of her own beside her by then. Someone strong, kind, reliable and loving. Not a serial womaniser who used people then dumped them.

Out of Greg's frying pan, she thought, her throat tightening, into Jake's fire. Potentially, a far more damaging experience.

Belle-laide, she thought. Graham had meant it kindly, but it wasn't the most flattering description.

Oh God, what had Jake been thinking of? she asked herself unhappily. Why hadn't he picked someone who looked the part, at least? Why on earth had he chosen her?

Because you, said an inconvenient voice in her head, know this weekend is business, not personal, and that he trusts you to take the money and walk away afterwards, without causing him unnecessary aggravation.

Yes, she thought. But only she would ever know that his trust could be misplaced.

Because when she'd been showering before lunch, standing under the torrent of water, she'd allowed her thoughts to drift. To imagine that she wasn't alone, that she felt the warmth of someone's breath on the nape of her neck and hands touching her, applying the scented gel to her skin, stroking its fragrance into her breasts, her stomach, her thighs. Caressing her gently.

Jake's hands...

Then paused, startled and ashamed, as she'd been forced to put out a hand to steady herself against the cubicle's tiled wall; her legs had suddenly been shaking under her, matching the race of her heart and the fierce, heated trembling that was at the same time building inside her. As her senses shivered in renewed arousal at the remembrance of his kiss, the hard, lithe strength of his body and the warm, clean scent of his skin. Emotions—responses she'd never experienced before or wished to indulge in. Because no other man she'd ever met, however decent and attractive he might be, had offered the least incentive for her to do so.

Now, as the memory came back to haunt her, Marin lifted her glass and drank deeply, trying to ease the dryness of her mouth as she felt her skin beginning to burn all over again, and a deep, yearning ache twist in the pit of her stomach. Oh God, she thought, her throat tightening. Why did it have to be Jake Radley-Smith of all people in the world who was making her feel like this?

But she had one shred of comfort. At least Jake didn't—couldn't, know the sensations he'd ignited in her hitherto unawakened flesh. She'd managed to conceal the fact that she was still quivering inwardly and give him an impersonal smile when he'd knocked at her door earlier to escort her to lunch.

She could only pray that he'd assume her un-guarded response to his kiss that morning was simply role-playing. That she'd been actually doing something to earn the promised money, trying to stop the plan coming off the rails.

He and Graham were still at the golf course when she eventually got back to the house. The croquet tournament was still in full swing, to judge from the laughter intermingled with cries of triumph and despair coming from the lawn, so she was able to escape up to her room unnoticed.

She felt hot, sticky and generally on edge, so she indulged herself with a long, cool bath then anointed herself all over with the achingly expensive scented moisturiser which Lynne had insisted on and, more cautiously, the perfume that matched it. It had a soft, musky fragrance with under-notes of lily and jasmine that were released slowly by the warmth of her skin, and it was far more beguiling and sophisticated than anything she'd possessed before.

Frankly sexy, in fact, she realised uncomfortably as she tried to relax on her bed. An impression that the evening's designated dress would do nothing to dispel.

Lynne had been right about the colour, she ac-knowledged ruefully, when later she looked at herself in the mirror after a life and death struggle to get the zip fastened.

The rose-leaf-green taffeta made her creamy skin glow in sensuous contrast, and added sparks of emerald to her hazel eyes. While the stark cut of the *bustier* managed somehow to enhance the slight curves it only just concealed.

My God, Marin thought, caught between laughter and shock. For the first time in my life, I have a cleavage.

She'd thought about swirling her hair up into a topknot, but decided she'd look slightly less naked if she let it hang in a soft and shining swathe round her shoulders. Her high-heeled sandals were simply a couple of green, sequined straps across the instep, and her tiny evening purse matched them.

And once more she was deliberately sparing in her use of cosmetics, merely darkening her long lashes and using a soft, pink lustre on her mouth. She had no wish to look as if she was trying too hard, she thought wryly.

Now it was again time to go downstairs and pretend. Except that the terms of this pretence had suddenly changed, and she was no longer sure exactly whom she was trying to fool.

It might even be—myself, she thought, swallowing.

She took one final look in the mirror, unease warring inside her with something that could easily be the wrong kind of excitement, then walked over to the communicating door.

She'd heard Jake return almost two hours before, and had half-expected a visit from him, but there'd only been silence from his room.

She knocked and was about to call, 'I'm ready,' when the door swung abruptly open and he confronted her.

She'd never seen him before in the formal elegance of dinner jacket and black tie, and realised just in time that she was actually gaping at him, her breath catching at his sheer glamour.

Jake looked her over in his turn for a long moment, his face inscrutable. When he spoke, his voice was light, even faintly amused. 'As well as the raise, I must remember to give Lynne a very large bonus.'

'She deserves it.' Marin tried to match his tone, although her pulses were going haywire. 'I fought her every step of the way.'

His mouth twisted. 'I can well believe it.' He let his gaze travel down her again from the wary, dark-fringed eyes to the length of slender leg revealed by the brief bell of her skirt. 'You look almost as enticing as you did in that towel you wore at our first meeting.'

Her face warmed. 'Something,' she said, 'that I have tried very hard to forget.'

'Now, there we differ,' Jake drawled. 'Because I suspect it will always feature amongst my most cherished memories.'

'Oh, please.' Marin lifted her chin. 'In a week's time we'll have problems remembering each other's names, and you know it.'

'Perhaps.' He shrugged. 'But it would hardly be chivalrous of me to say so.'

'I wasn't aware chivalry featured highly on your list of priorities, anyway.'

His mouth twisted mockingly. 'I'm probably capable of it, if the situation demands.' He paused. 'Now, shall we go downstairs—face the lions in the arena one more time?'

She thought— But there are far worse things than lions....

Aloud, she said sedately, 'Let them do their worst.'

And walked beside him in silence down to the drawing room.

CHAPTER SEVEN

IT PROBABLY WASN'T the worst evening she'd ever spent, Marin thought detachedly, but it was high on the list.

Diana had rounded up all the local grandees for the dinner, including the Chief Constable, but Marin gathered that other people had been invited later for dancing, and that a disco run by the doctor's student son had been set up in the large conservatory at the rear of the house.

In the dining room, she'd found herself next to Chaz Stratton, who confined himself to telling her that she wouldn't have found the croquet contest quite so easy, and that Diana had won.

Marin murmured politely, thinking how much she'd like to take his vichyssoise and upend it into his lap.

On her other side was the local Member of Parliament, a thin, greyish man who clearly preferred monologues conducted by himself to conversation, so she was required to do little but listen and try not to let her glance stray too obviously or wistfully to where Jake was sitting, being animatedly entertained by a very attractive brunette.

It occurred to her that this was what it must be like to be Jake's girlfriend in reality. To be another Adela Mason, always wondering if every other woman in the room was a potential rival, and if so how to deal with it. Or to accept, like the unknown Celia Forrest, that Jake did not play for keeps and walk away before the inevitable happened.

And found she was putting down her dessert spoon, her appetite for floating island pudding suddenly replaced by a tight knot of unhappiness in her chest.

Finding herself overtaken by the startling and appalling realisation that no amount of money could ever make up for the kind of wretchedness that was going to be waiting for her once the weekend was over.

Oh God, she thought, swallowing. How can I have allowed this to happen to me? And let it get to this stage?

It wasn't just her first confrontation with actual sexual temptation, or finding herself in close proximity to a diabolically attractive and experienced man. If that was so, she might have found some means of dealing with it.

But it was no longer as simple as that. In some devastating way, her heart and her head had somehow become involved too, so that her often-repeated mantra. 'All over soon'—was no longer reassurance but a cry of pain.

And the knowledge of that scared her half to death.

She was suddenly, startlingly aware, without even glancing in his direction, that Jake was no longer looking at his companion but at her. Knew, too, that if she met his gaze she might not have the sophistication to hide her inner tumult from his perception.

Keeping her eyes fixed resolutely on the table, she thought—I shall have to be so careful. So desperately careful.

It was a relief when the meal ended and the other guests started to arrive.

Marin's plan was to get lost once more in the general melee, and maybe beat a strategic retreat back to her room, only to realise she was no longer wearing her usual protective camouflage, and that the younger crowd who'd now joined the party were homing in on her and sweeping her along to where the music was already playing.

It was a while since she'd been dancing, but she soon discovered that her natural grace and rhythm had not deserted her. And if the frankly appreciative comments about her appearance from her various partners were a little embarrassing, they were also gratifying. Especially when Diana had greeted her earlier with the kind of look usually accorded to an earwig lurking in a salad.

She'd imagined that the party would divide, with Graham and his older guests remaining in the drawing room, but she was entirely wrong. The beat of the music seemed to act like a magnet for everyone.

She caught a glimpse of Jake partnering his

brunette, and deliberately turned to take him out of her line of vision.

He's doing the right thing, she told herself defensively. She's glamorous and sophisticated—all the things I'm not—and no one in the world would be the least bit surprised if he moved on to her. Even Diana Halsay would have to believe it, and admit defeat.

I just didn't expect it to happen like this, or so soon. But I have no grounds for complaint. All I can do is put up and shut up, because that's what I'm being paid for.

In the meantime, the music was a shield for her to hide behind, and if her smile felt as if it had been nailed on, and her brain ached with the effort of being pleasant to all these strangers and forcing herself to flirt back, she was the only one who knew it.

Until, inevitably, the amateur DJ decided to change the mood and the music softened and slowed into dreaminess, encouraging the gyrating couples to move closer, even to touch.

And suddenly Jake was beside her.

He said softly, 'I think this is our dance,' and made to take her in his arms.

For a moment she looked at him almost dazedly as an anguished voice inside her head began whispering, 'I can't do this—I can't let him hold me as if I'm the one he truly wants to be near. I can't slow-dance with him and feel his lips against my hair, my face; I couldn't bear it. It's a pretence too far...'

She stepped back, forcing another smile, even managing to make it rueful this time. 'Jake, I'm really sorry, but I'm afraid you're going to have to excuse me. I'm—all partied out and falling asleep on my feet, so I've decided to call it a night.'

There was an odd silence, then Jake said courteously, 'Yes, darling, of course. I quite understand. I'll try not to disturb you when I come up.'

'Thank you,' she said. 'That would be—kind.' She looked around her, smiled again rather waveringly, said a general goodnight and tried not to make it too obvious that she was in flight.

She was breathless when she reached her room. Breathless, and suddenly close to tears. Fiercely, she fought them back as she closed the door, leaning back against its panels.

'Get a grip,' she adjured herself harshly, and aloud. 'If this is how you are after forty-eight hours with him, what the hell would you be like after a week? This is sheer self-preservation you're doing here.'

Someone had been up as usual to turn down her bed, light the lamp on the night table and draw the curtains. Her window had been left open, and the folds of chintz were stirring in the slight breeze, which also brought all too clearly the sweet, seductive sound of the music below.

Something she definitely didn't need, she thought, crossing the room and pulling the casement shut with a sharp jerk, trying hard at the same time not to wonder if Jake had returned to his brunette.

That, she told herself, is not your business. And you'd be better occupied concentrating on that unfinished list of stuff for Essex than indulging in useless and damaging speculation.

But first, she decided, slipping off her sandals and flexing her toes, she would get undressed and into bed. Not that she was tired. Not yet.

Restless, she thought. Edgy. That's me. But a night's sleep will get me back on track.

She took one last look in the mirror to say a faintly regretful goodbye to the flushed, dishevelled stranger in the sexy dress, then reached round to undo her zip. Only to discover, after several minutes of determined tugging, that it was refusing to move as much as a millimetre.

Marin, remembering the difficulties of fastening it when she was dressing, gave a silent groan.

Think, she told herself robustly. Use some logic. If you can twist the dress round somehow so the zip's at the front, you'll at least be able to see what the problem is and have a chance of dealing with it.

But this soon proved to be wishful thinking. The tight *bustier* clung to her as if it was a second skin and refused to budge in any other direction.

She said aloud, 'Oh, this is ludicrous.' The dress might have transformed her for a couple of hours, but she had no wish to spend the rest of the night in it. Or, for choice, even another five minutes.

Taking a deep breath, she tried the zip again, holding the edge of the dress firmly with her other hand, pleading silently as she tried to coax the little metal tongue downwards. But all to no avail.

She wanted very badly to jump up and down screaming, but restrained herself. Losing one's temper with inanimate objects was a waste of time. She needed patience and perseverance instead.

Or someone to help. Well, one person, and he wasn't there. He hadn't followed her upstairs tonight, she thought, her throat tightening. She was on her own.

Half an hour later, her arms aching, she gave up the fight. She walked over to the bed and lay down on top of it, first carefully smoothing the taffeta skirt to avoid undue creasing. Then she switched off her lamp and resolutely closed her eyes.

She was almost dozing when she heard the sound of a door shutting. She sat up, staring at the thin thread of light visible from the next room, then slid off the bed, trod barefoot across the carpet and knocked.

There was a brief pause, then the door opened and Jake confronted her. She realised she must have heard him returning from the bathroom, because he was wearing a towelling robe and his hair was damp, indicating that in spite of the lateness of the hour he'd taken a shower.

He looked her over, unsmiling. 'You gave the impression downstairs that you were worn out,' he said. 'So why aren't you in bed and fast asleep?'

She lifted her chin. 'Because I can't get my dress off. The zip's stuck.'

Jake shrugged, his mouth hard. 'Then ring the bell for Mrs Martin. Get her to bring some scissors and cut you out of it.'

'At this time of night?' Marin stared at him. 'When we're supposed to be lovers on terms of total intimacy? Wouldn't you be the one I'd naturally turn to first? The only one?' She shook her head. 'Unless, of course, you want to confirm to Diana that there really is nothing between us. Because that's what she'll think when she hears about it—and it will probably be served up with her morning tea.'

She paused. 'Besides, I don't want it simply—hacked off me. Do you know what it cost?'

'No,' he said. 'It's not that important.'

'Well, it is to me. It's far too beautiful a dress to damage.' *And for the first time in my life I felt beautiful, wearing it. And desirable.*

She added, her voice uneven, 'Couldn't you at least try to free the zip for me before the whole thing has to be ruined?'

'Slight problem there,' he said curtly. 'It would mean I'd have to touch you.'

'That doesn't matter…'

'It bloody well mattered when I wanted to dance with you a while ago,' he retorted. 'Or did you think I wouldn't know?'

Her throat tightened. She made herself shrug lightly. 'You seemed to be having such a good time, I was merely trying to be tactful.'

His brows rose. 'You mean, the lovely Vanessa?' he asked sardonically. 'Divorced, available and a last-minute addition to the guest list, as she artlessly revealed over the soup? Who'd arrived by taxi but was *so* hoping for a lift home? That Vanessa?'

He gave an impatient sigh. 'For God's sake, Marin, it was Diana trying to set me up. Couldn't you see that? God help me, I was sending out Mayday signals to you from the middle of dinner, but you were clearly too busy to notice, so I was stuck with her.'

'Not many men would have found her company a hardship,' she said defiantly.

'I'm sure that's true,' Jake agreed politely. 'She was certainly easy on the eye, and eager to please. Unfortunately, she was also drenched in my least favourite scent. I was still reeking of it when I came upstairs, which is why I took a shower.' He paused. 'In case you were wondering.'

'I wasn't,' Marin said. It was her turn to hesitate. 'But why would Mrs Halsay do such a thing?'

He shrugged again. 'I presume in order to demonstrate to her husband that I'm still an unreliable, womanising bastard not safe to be allowed near any good-looking woman,' he returned caustically. 'And your sudden retired—hurt departure wouldn't have helped matters, either,' he added with a touch of grimness. 'You'd certainly get the sympathy vote from a lot of people.'

'I wasn't looking for that.' She gestured helplessly. 'I don't expect you to understand, but I'd just had enough.'

His mouth tightened. 'I know the feeling.' He paused. 'Now turn round and I'll see what I can do with that zip.' As she obeyed, he added curtly, 'I suggest you breathe in very deeply. And keep still.'

Easier said than done, she thought, when her whole being seemed to be shivering, anticipating the first brush of his hand against her skin. But maybe by dint of tensing every muscle and holding her breath at the same time she might be able to hide the deep inner trembling she could neither deny nor control—at least for a moment or two.

She felt his warm breath stir the soft tendrils of hair on the nape of her neck as he hooked his fingers into the back of her dress, easing it carefully away from her body.

He gave a quiet whistle. 'You seem to have caught half the lining,' he commented. 'Maybe we should admit defeat and send for those scissors.' He waited for a moment, then added. 'Unless you really want me to try.'

She said, dry-mouthed, 'Yes.' And then, 'Please.'

Realising for the first time, as she did so, exactly what she was inviting. And knowing with mingled shame and excitement that she would not change a thing.

It was sheer torment, she soon realised, to stand there feeling his cool fingers moving against her naked spine.

Although, admittedly, there was nothing remotely sexual in his touch. He was simply doing what he'd been asked, no more.

But the aching, quivering sensations inside her that seemed to be spreading to every nerve-ending she possessed told her that it was enough. Even—too much.

Hidden in the folds of her skirt, her hands were curling into fists, the nails scoring the soft palms as she fought to maintain the semblance of outward control.

Jake said, 'Let's see…' Then, 'Ah,' on a note of quiet triumph as the zip moved down a little.

He added, 'Can you hold your breath for me once more?'

She said, 'No problem.'

Nor was it, she thought, because it gave her the perfect excuse to be breathless afterwards, for her voice to sound husky.

'Right.' He paused. 'I'll be as quick as I can.'

His hand was right inside her dress now, tugging at the imprisoned fabric, and she stood, braced and motionless, feeling the zip edging down little by little as he freed it.

He said, 'That's it,' and the zip slid down unhampered to its fullest extent and Marin grabbed at the front of her dress to prevent that slipping too.

She should step away, she told herself. Thank him politely for his help, say goodnight and—part, closing the door between them.

Jake's hands lifted, lightly clasping her bare shoulders, his thumbs smoothing her skin, tracing the delicate bone structure. He'd moved closer too, making her suddenly, startlingly conscious of the heat of his body against her exposed back.

Now was the moment to speak, she thought with a kind of desperation. To end this while it was still possible for her to do so. Before all that she was feeling—wanting—overwhelmed her.

Because she did not do things like this. It was a principle, a cornerstone of how she lived. Or was it simply that she had never before known real temptation? Real desire?

And now that she knew, her whole being was crying out for fulfilment by the man who had awakened her to fulfilment's possibilities. Because this might be her only chance for it to happen.

One night, she thought, her mind suddenly reeling. One night. Oh God, is that really so much to ask?

His fingers brushed her hair away from her neck, and she felt his lips touch its tender nape, moving slowly—easily, on her skin. It was the lightest of pressures, like the brush of a butterfly's wing, but it made her whole being shiver with instinctive, uncontrollable longing.

But as her back arched helplessly, achingly, in response, Jake took his hands from her shoulders, swiftly and deliberately setting her free again.

For an instant, she stood motionless, still holding

the boned taffeta bodice over her breasts. Then her body's urgency—need—took over and she let the dress slip down, baring her to the waist, then to the hips, until finally it slid to the floor and she stepped out of it.

She turned slowly to face him, her silk and lace briefs her only covering.

Jake looked back at her, his expression totally arrested, the lines of his cheekbones, his mouth and jaw sharply, even starkly delineated, the blue eyes burning.

He took an unsteady breath, then began to shake his head, his lips shaping a word she knew would be 'No.'

With a little sob, she flung herself towards him, her entire body one desperate plea. As she pressed herself against him, the towelling robe grazed her hardening nipples, sending a sharp ache of longing coursing like wildfire through her veins. And deep within her she felt her muscles clench almost savagely.

Her arms reached up round his neck, drawing him down to her and to the first kiss she had ever offered him of her own accord.

His mouth found hers, exploring its trembling contours without haste. Possessing them, as one hand twined in the soft fall of her hair, letting it slide through his fingers as they kissed. The other hand clasped her hip, pulling her closer as his lips parted hers, his tongue delicately, sensuously probing her moist, inner sweetness.

He raised his head at last, looking down at her, turning her slightly so that she was leaning back in his arms as he planted a trail of kisses down the line of her neck and into the vulnerable hollows at its base, making her pulse leap and dance.

His hand found one soft breast and cupped it, teasing the awakened and quivering peak with a fingertip before taking the small, scented mound gently into his mouth and continuing the delicious torment with his tongue, forcing a gasp from her throat at this unaccustomed, bewildering delight.

At the same time, his hand strayed lightly down her slenderness, whispering over her skin, discovering without haste every slender curve, angle and hollow, and as he did so brushing away the last fragile barrier to his total exploration of her.

Marin swayed in his arms, eyes closed, her uncovered body totally pliant, the breath catching in her throat as his fingers reached her thighs, gently stroking the silken inner flesh before beginning a more intimate quest. A small stifled cry, half protest, half hunger, escaped her as for the first time in her life she experienced a man's touch like cool gossamer against the scalding heat of her. Her body moved, lifting instinctively, helplessly in response to the subtle pressure of his caress, and she felt the melting rush of a desire as wanton as it was unfamiliar.

Her legs suddenly seemed unable to support her and she caught at the lapel of his robe, trying to steady herself, shocked at her unguarded flesh's primitive reaction to its first real experience of carnality. To the sweet, languorous weakness which seemed to be invading her entire being.

Jake said her name, his own voice hardly more than a sigh as he picked her up in his arms and carried her into his room. To his bed.

She felt the softness of the pillows at her back, the crispness of the sheets against her skin. But as he began to take off his robe Marin turned away quickly, reaching for the switch of the single lamp glowing on the night table, her inherent shyness tightening her throat at the thought of seeing him naked, and in reality instead of imagination.

Of actually being with him naked.

But Jake was too quick for her, leaning across as he lay down beside her to capture her wrist and bring her hand back to his body, flattening it against his chest, the swift thud of his heart mirroring her own accelerated pulse rate.

He whispered, 'Sweetheart, I need to see you. To look into your eyes. And I need you to see me too.'

And, gathering her to him, he kissed her again, his mouth irresistibly demanding as it moved on hers, the force of his erection hard against her thighs.

Sensation crowded upon her, making her dizzy. The cool beguiling scent of his skin was all around her, the taut muscularity of his shoulders beneath her hands as she held him, returning his kisses with undreamed-of urgency.

Jake let his lips drift slowly down her throat to her breasts, suckling them gently as his tongue resumed its delectable arousal of their rosebud peaks. She felt the throb of aching need reverberating through her whole body, echoing deep in her loins, and she put a fist to her mouth, damming back the tiny, betraying sounds that would reveal the depths of her craving for him.

His mouth moved downward, across her breathless midriff to the satin of her belly and the indentation of her navel, his tongue tracing its whorls with minute accuracy.

His hands slipped down her body, moulding her slim hips then sliding beneath them, cupping her buttocks as he raised her towards him so he could kiss her thighs and rub his cheek lingeringly against their smoothness. Before bending to her again with new and devastating purpose.

Marin could hear the thunder of her quickened heartbeat as a small, frantic voice in her head told her, no, this couldn't be happening. He would not, could not, really be intending to…

Because, if so, she must stop him now—now…

Or it would be too late.…

Only to feel his mouth warm and sensuous as it caressed the silken mound at the joining of her thighs, silently coaxing her legs to part and allow him the ultimate access he sought. Making her realise that denial was no longer an option, even if she could force some kind of protest from her dry throat.

And then all thinking halted, her mind going into free fall as she allowed him to have his way. She became aware of nothing but the devastating mastery of his tongue as it flickered on her, seeking her tiny nub of sensitive flesh, teasing it until it had swollen into an agony of total sensation.

Then, just when she thought she could bear no more, finding that his caress had changed. That he was now skilfully laving and stroking all the burning, secret places of her womanhood, probing their slick, moist depths, making her writhe beneath him in a ferment of sensation bordering on anguish.

Just before he returned slowly and quite deliberately to her little erect bud, tantalising it softly to a renewed pitch of intensity that she had not realised could exist or that she could possibly experience.

Before he drew her with an infinity of expertise to some unimagined brink and held her there as her head thrashed on the pillow and a silent scream rose in her throat.

Before, between one heartbeat and the next, he finally took her across the edge into the unknown. The unbelievable.

Her amazed body arched beneath his mouth as the first throbbing convulsions of a pleasure that was almost pain imploded inside her. She heard herself cry out loud, a harsh, broken sound, her body shaking uncontrollably with the violence of the spasms tearing through her as they reached their zenith, then began by degrees to subside.

CHAPTER EIGHT

WHEN IT WAS over, Marin lay very still, her body limp and slackened, trying to comprehend what had just happened to her but failing utterly.

To tell herself she'd reached her first climax would do no kind of justice to the incredible, irresistible force Jake had released in her. Or his skill in achieving it, she thought, her body blooming with warmth.

She felt him move, raise himself above her and look down into her dazed, incredulous eyes. His own gaze was faintly questioning, and she responded silently, lifting a hand to touch his still-damp hair and stroke his face, running her fingers almost wonderingly over the slight shadowing of stubble along his jawline.

Jake captured her hand and brought it to his lips, caressing its palm, then grazing the soft mound at the base of her thumb with his teeth, and she felt the enticement of it shiver sweetly through her nerve-endings.

He took her hand back to his chest, back to the harsh rhythm of his heartbeat. He whispered, 'Touch me,' and lay back against the pillows, his eyes half-closed, waiting for her.

At first, her compliance was hesitant, but gradually, as she discovered the marvellous strength of bone structure and play of muscle under her fingertips, she forgot everything but the overwhelming need to know him. To learn and enjoy the texture of his skin and the planes, angles and curves of his lean, firm body. To hear him sigh with pleasure as her hands became more confident, more daring, until finally she reached his loins and the jutting male strength of him, her hands trembling as she clasped him, fondling him gently, aware that her own excitement was starting to build again. The memory of her own delight still potent, she bent her head, caressing him shyly with her lips.

'Darling.' His voice was a hoarse groan. 'Oh Christ, my sweet...'

He moved, lifting himself over her. Started with immense care to enter her, easing his way into the wet, yielding heat of her willing flesh.

She felt a brief, burning pressure, and gasped. Felt him pause, sensing her sudden tension and, knowing that he could not—must not stop, she grasped his shoulders, raising herself towards him in blind and total surrender. Offering herself to the one long, controlled thrust that sheathed him in her with utter completeness, the pain of her body's resistance over almost as soon as it had begun.

When it was done, Jake stayed very still, his blue gaze quietly watchful, as if anticipating some other sign of reluctance or discomfort from her. And she looked back at him, wanting to let him know that she was ready and more than willing to give him everything he wanted from her. And smiled, breathing his name.

He bent his head, kissing her smile with his own, and began to move in her, his loins barely rocking against hers in the gentlest of motions. Marin felt the sweetness of this new rhythm in her blood, her bones. Found her response to it as natural, as necessary as drawing her next breath. But was bewildered by it just the same, because it wasn't what she'd expected.

Of course, what she knew about men and their behaviour during sex was less than minimal, she reminded herself as her breathing quickened helplessly, but she'd imagined rather more—urgency would be involved in his need for satisfaction.

'What's the matter?' Jake asked softly.

Her voice was a small, husky croak. 'I don't understand. Don't you want to…?'

'Very much,' he said. 'But I'm waiting for you.'

'For me?' Marin stared up at him. 'But I won't— I couldn't…' She broke off, her colour deepening helplessly.

'No?' He was smiling again as he shifted, subtly altering his position, his movement inside her slow and smooth but at the same time more forceful. His mouth was warm and lingering on her parted, astonished lips. Hot and demanding on the hardening excitement of her nipples.

He pushed more deeply into her, withdrew a little,

then pushed again, reaching some secret place far inside her and creating another kind of new and exquisite sensation there with an erotic mastery that had her twisting helplessly under him, her mind and will wiped of everything but the wicked, beautiful things his body was doing to hers.

There. *There...*

She said, her voice drowning, 'Oh, God, no—no,' as she felt the first quivers of ecstatic abandonment rippling within her, then building fiercely to their inexorable crescendo, her muscles clenching powerfully around him.

And heard Jake's harsh groans of rapture as he at last allowed himself to attain his own release.

She was aware of quietude and a profound peace. Of lying still wrapped in his arms, their bodies joined, his dark head against her breasts. Of sudden, unexpected tears on her face.

And, as if he was aware of this last reaction, he separated from her with the same care he'd used in his possession of her, gently drying her wet face with a corner of the sheet then stroking her dishevelled hair as he held her, his voice a soothing murmur.

Eventually, she said, mumbling, 'I'm not sad—really, I'm not.'

'I'm glad to hear it.' He kissed her eyes and her lips.

'I wanted you to know that.' She tried to stifle a yawn and failed. 'Oh God,' she added, mortified. 'I'm so sorry.'

'Don't be.' He switched off the lamp and drew her close to him, pillowing her head on his chest. 'We could both do with some sleep.'

Sleep? thought Marin. How could she possibly do that with everything that had just happened still churning in her mind?

Especially when she'd never shared a bed before with anyone before—let alone a man.

But she hadn't expected to find his warm body so comfortable to relax against, or the resonance of his heartbeat under her cheek so soothing, she told herself with a little contented sigh. And slept.

A pale, grey light was beginning to penetrate the room when she opened her eyes. For a moment Marin lay still, slightly disorientated, aware of little more than the delicious lassitude permeating her entire being, wondering drowsily what had disturbed her slumber.

Then she turned her head slowly and saw Jake propped up on one elbow, watching her, and realised with a lift of her heart that she'd been woken by the touch of his lips.

'Hey,' he said softly. 'Remember me?'

She stretched languidly, deliberately, observing the flare of his blue gaze as the covering sheet slipped down her body. She pretended to frown.

'I'm not altogether sure. Maybe you could—jog my memory?'

'With pleasure.' His hand cupped her breast, the

ball of his thumb rubbing slowly across the nipple. 'Does that strike a chord?'

'Mmm,' she murmured thoughtfully. 'Something seems to be stirring in the back of my mind.'

'Is that all?' There was a quiver of open amusement in his voice as he let his hand slide down her body to the soft mound at the junction of her thighs. 'Maybe—this will be more help…'

It was suddenly difficult to breathe or even to think as his fingers caressed her, lightly, teasingly. She managed, 'If you could be—a little more specific…'

And made a sound between a laugh and a sob of delight as he pulled her towards him, under him, raising her legs to lock round him as he entered her.

Impossible, she thought, her senses in free fall as she clung to his shoulders, that she could be so ready for him. Impossible, even shameful, that she should be so eager—so hungry, enclosing him in her moist and willing heat, as her body offered the counterpoint to each firm and powerful thrust that was carrying her away with him to heaven.

Even so he made her wait, keeping her balanced for an eternity on some knife-edge of trembling desire before driving her into the harsh sweetness of orgasm. And when she cried out, her voice ragged, she heard him answer her.

She slept again, wrapped in his arms, and awoke to the first streaks of sunrise. They had moved a little apart at some point, and Marin turned on to her side, letting her eyes explore every detail of the magnificent, naked body sprawled beside her. The first time, she realised, she had ever really looked at him. Or had the leisure to do so, she conceded, a mischievous smile curving her lips.

Her first hint that he was awake and fully aware of her fascinated scrutiny was his politely uttered, 'Good morning.'

She jumped guiltily. 'Thank you. And an even better one to you.' She paused. 'So—you do have an all-over tan.'

His eyes opened and he lifted a lazy brow. 'You mean, you'd actually wondered?' he asked and grinned. 'Life just gets better.'

'No,' she protested too hastily. 'No, of course not.'

His smile widened. 'Fibber.' He rolled over, pulling her towards him and kissing her on the tip of her nose. 'Whereas you, my virtuous angel, have clearly been wearing a bikini at some recent date—even if you wouldn't do so this weekend. And it covered you from here…' He trailed his lips across the swell of her breasts just above her nipples. 'To there.' His tongue traced her cleavage and beyond.

'And from here,' he added, skimming a finger from the curve of one hip to the other. 'Down to—here.' He paused, lingering, deliberately tantalising. 'So—what colour was it?'

She swallowed, her skin warming helplessly at his touch. 'Why do you want to know?'

'So I can imagine taking it off,' Jake whispered, and began to kiss her again.

Afterwards he slept again, one arm thrown across her, but she could not. The room was golden with sunshine now, and she felt part of it, part of all that warmth and promise, her perceptions heightened—coloured by what had happened to her here. Her body felt entirely different too, her skin seeming to tingle—to glow.

Nor was it because she was quite definitely aching a little. More than a little, if she was really honest.

And, more prosaically, she was hungry.

Careful not to disturb him, she slid from under his imprisoning arm and tiptoed across to her room, retrieving her dress and briefs *en route* and putting them away.

Then, picking out a straight, white linen skirt, a silky black top and some underwear, she went into the bathroom. She filled the tub with warm water, adding fragrant bath-oil, and sank into it with a sigh of contentment.

She thought, I've lost my virginity. And paused, because that was hardly an accurate description of what had transpired last night.

'I didn't lose a thing,' she told herself defiantly. 'I gave it away, freely, willingly and quite gloriously.'

The kind of behaviour she'd always secretly condemned. And yet she didn't regret a thing. How could she?

In retrospect it had not been exactly what she'd anticipated, mainly because she'd not expected him to be quite so considerate—so gentle. From what she'd gleaned from the giggled conversations of female colleagues, it had seemed that men, carried away in the throes of passion, could behave very differently.

And she wondered if, perhaps, Jake had made allowances for her ignorance of what really turned men on.

She sat up abruptly. What the hell was she thinking? Was she deliberately trying to tarnish the sheer magic of what had happened between them?

It was wonderful, she thought. And he made it wonderful. There was no more to it than that.

Half an hour later, bathed and dressed, she went to his door and peeped in to see if he was awake, but he hadn't stirred, so she made her way downstairs alone.

She could hear the buzz of conversation from the dining room, and knew suddenly that food could wait. That she didn't want to see anyone just yet.

That she wanted to hug last night and its secrets to her a little longer.

She went through the drawing room and out on to the terrace, standing by the balustrade and looking out over the gardens. The lawns looked particularly inviting, she thought, as if they were waiting for her to dance across them—or turn a cartwheel for sheer joy.

Her face splintered into a grin. 'As if,' she told herself, and turned to go back in the house, nearly cannoning into Diana Halsay, who was standing right behind her.

'Well, well,' Diana said softly. 'You look very pleased with yourself this morning. Has Jake taken pity on you at last?' Her eyes swept Marin from head to foot in a piercing assessment. 'Why, I do believe that he has.' She laughed. 'Not just *belle-laide* any more, but well and truly laid, if I'm any judge.'

Marin said, 'I don't know what you mean.' Only to be totally betrayed by the bright wave of colour that was sweeping from her toes up to the roots of her hair, making her burn with humiliation under the other's all-knowing gaze.

'I suppose it was inevitable,' Diana went on, musing. 'Even though it may not have been what he intended originally.

'You see, I was never fooled by that "here's my new girlfriend" routine. Graham may think it's love, that Jake's met his fate at last, but we three know that isn't true—don't we? That it's all just a clever trick to get the sexy Mr Radley-Smith off the hook—the ultimate PR spin.'

She shrugged. 'I suppose you hinted to Jake that I didn't believe it. Making him realise he might need to take—stronger measures to make his little deception really plausible.

'And you weren't exactly unwilling, were you, my dear? Or subtle about what you wanted. In fact, everyone noticed how you've been trailing after him all weekend with your tongue hanging out. As Sylvia said, like a starving kid outside a baker's window. And Jake, like a perfect gentleman, has duly obliged, thus killing two birds with one stone. So in one way you owe me a vote of thanks, or he might never have bothered.'

There was sudden nausea, hot and bitter, in Marin's throat. She swallowed. 'How—how dare you talk to me like this? I refuse to listen to any more.'

'How very disappointing,' Diana said brightly. 'When at last we have something in common to discuss.' She paused, a little smile curling her mouth. 'He's good, isn't he?' She lowered her voice intimately, sister to sister, talking about a pleasure shared. 'Knows all the right buttons to press, as it were. I'm sure he rewarded you very generously for being such a good girl.'

She gave a little gurgle of laughter. 'However, I presume he wasn't in one of his more adventurous moods, or you probably wouldn't be able to walk this morning.'

Marin was shaking, but she managed to lift her chin. 'You're crude,' she said with quiet clarity. 'Crude and unbelievably vile.'

'And you, Miss Wade, are a fool,' Diana retorted, shrugging. 'Oh, I expect you'll be enough of a novelty to become the flavour of the month for a little while.' She shrugged. 'After all, I'm sure he's grateful if nothing else. But he also gets bored very easily—and very quickly. He'll soon have exhausted all your limited possibilities.

'And he certainly doesn't do happy-ever-after, in case you were hoping.'

'I wasn't.' Marin's voice was ice, chipped from the shivering emptiness inside her. 'But thanks for your concern, if that's what it is. Goodbye, Mrs Halsay.'

She walked past Diana into the house, heading blindly across the drawing room and out into the hall to the downstairs cloakroom, her heart beating like a wild creature chased by hunters.

She shot the small, brass bolt on the door, then walked across to the tiled vanity unit with its scented soaps, hand lotions and pile of small, fluffy towels. Leaning over the shell-shaped basin, she retched drily and weakly.

As the feeling of nausea began to pass and she felt marginally calmer, she straightened, turning on the cold tap and letting the water run over the pulses in her wrists. She caught her reflection in the large gilt-edged mirror right in front of her.

Found herself looking at—understanding—what Diana Halsay had seen: all the signs of self-betrayal. The shadowed, dreaming eyes emphasised by the smudges of sleeplessness beneath them; the sensuous, luminous pallor of her skin and the soft mouth, blurred and swollen with kissing.

Well and truly laid. Diana's words ate into her brain like acid. Corrosive, destructive.

Has Jake taken pity on you at last? Like a starving kid outside a baker's window.

Comments that made her feel as if the skin had

been flayed from her body. Because she could not deny that they held a basic truth.

I thought I'd been so clever, she thought, pretending to pretend, hiding what I was truly feeling. But I was only fooling myself. And all the time people have been laughing at me.

She poured water into her cupped hands, splashing it on to her face as if she could wash away the evidence of last night. Of her appalling weakness. Her stupidity. That, she thought, above all.

And now she had to go back and face them, the occupants of this small, malicious world, and the man who'd brought her here. Subjected her to this. The man she now had to rely on to take her out of it and back to where she really belonged, she reminded herself bitterly.

And quelled the sob rising in her throat.

The dining room was mercifully empty. There was coffee on a hot-plate on the sideboard and she poured some into a cup, swallowing it in great, painful gulps, trying to dispel the chill inside her.

She did not turn as she heard someone enter the room, but she knew instantly who it was, and her body tensed painfully.

Jake's arms slid round her waist, drawing her back against him as he nuzzled her neck. 'Where did you go?'

By some supreme effort, her voice sounded almost normal. 'I—I couldn't sleep.'

'You should have woken me.' He smiled against her skin. 'I know the perfect cure for insomnia.'

'Anyway, it was morning.' She remembered lying in his arms, watching night turn into day, her body glowing with joy and fulfilment. Making her forget that people spoke about 'the cold light of dawn'. Meaning a time when reason and commonsense kicked in. Even a time for an agony of shame and bitter regret.

'You speak as if that makes a difference,' he said softly. 'All evidence to the contrary.'

The words twisted inside her like a knife. She released herself. 'How—how soon can we leave here, please?'

'It's usual to stay for lunch,' he said after a pause. 'But we can go earlier, if that's what you want.'

'Yes.' Her voice shook a little. 'I—really want to. I—I've had enough.'

'Which makes two of us, believe me.'

Believe me. Oh God, how could he say that? she wondered, unable to look at him as he stood beside her, casually helping himself to coffee.

'You go and pack our things,' he went on. 'While I have a final brief word with Graham, and then we can be off.'

Marin was standing by her bedroom window, gazing sightlessly at the garden, some fifteen minutes later when she heard him go into his room. A moment later, he appeared in the doorway.

'You didn't pack for me?'

She turned defensively. 'I didn't know you wanted me to.' It was a lie. She couldn't bear the implied intimacy of handling his clothing, touching things he'd worn recently. Behaving as if they were a couple.

He shrugged, sending her a faintly puzzled look. 'It would have saved time, that's all. But it doesn't really matter.'

He paused. 'I've already said our farewells. Our hostess has swept her female guests off to the tennis court, and Graham and the guys are planning to play poker.'

He smiled at her. 'I'll throw my things together then, with one bound, we can be free.'

The garden blurred suddenly, but her voice was steady. 'Yes,' she said. 'We can.' And felt her heart break.

CHAPTER NINE

THE VILLAGE WAS several miles behind them. That part of her ordeal was over, but now she had to deal with its aftermath.

In spite of herself, she found she was glancing sideways at his hands on the wheel of the car as they steered it, controlled it, with effortless expertise.

Just as he'd done with her last night. His hands on her body touching, arousing, with the same precision. Taking her exactly where he wanted her to go.

And, God help her, she'd wanted it too. Had wanted all of it and more. Had wanted the glory of him with her, inside her, as they reached paradise together. Had prayed for it never to stop.

Only to find all that pain, hunger and rapture belittled—reduced to words like *pity*, *reward* and *gratitude*. The passion she'd imagined replaced by a sense of obligation.

He'd performed, she thought. He'd given her pleasure, because she'd made it so shamefully clear that was what she required. Why she'd thrown herself at him, as she had.

He knew how to arouse—to fulfil, but that did not mean that he had to be emotionally engaged. Inexperienced as she was, she'd been aware of his restraint. Maybe he'd simply known how little effort on his part would be needed to bring her to climax. Turn her into his willing creature.

Worst of all, she'd ignored the fact that he'd tried to step back from her.

Suddenly she remembered Greg, standing in the flat in France. 'She's no bloody oil-painting,' he'd said, the words dripping with contempt. 'Who the hell would want to start anything with such a pathetic little object?'

Oh God, she whispered under her breath. How can it be possible to hurt so much? To feel so ashamed?

'Well, that's that, thank God.' She started as Jake's voice intruded on her unhappy reverie. 'Would you mind if we made a slight detour?'

She swallowed. 'Why should we do that?'

'There's somewhere we could have lunch,' he said. There was a smile in his voice. 'It's not too far out of our way, and you might like it.'

'Thank you.' Her voice was polite but definite. 'But I'd rather go straight back to London. If you don't mind.'

She couldn't bear, she thought, to spend any more time with him than was strictly necessary. And once this journey was over she would never see him again.

'Well, just as you want,' he said after a pause.

'The other will keep, and maybe London is the best option at this point. How about I drop you at the flat to pack the rest of your stuff and collect you in an hour or so?'

'Collect me?' Marin repeated. Her head turned sharply towards him. 'What do you mean?'

'I live in Chelsea, darling,' he said. 'You don't imagine I'd suggest you get there by public transport?'

'I know where you live,' she said. 'How does it concern me?'

There was a silence, then Jake said quietly, 'I'd imagined it would concern you very closely.' He slowed the car, driving on to the broad grass verge, then braked and switched the engine off. He unfastened his seat belt and turned, frowning slightly as the blue eyes searched her face.

He said, 'You see, I thought—I hoped—that you'd be moving in with me.' He smiled faintly. 'After all, I can hardly come and live with you. Lynne would have a heart attack if she had to fight me for the shower each morning. Or if she found us in the bath together.'

The flavour of the month for a little while...

Pain twisted inside her as she recalled those other mocking words, which had told her nothing but the truth.

Instead, she moved suddenly, restively. 'You think I'm coming to live with you because of what happened last night?' She shook her head. 'That's—

over and done with. And now I have my own life to go back to. So I have no intention of sharing anyone else's, even on a temporary basis. I never did.'

His gaze sharpened. Became incredulous. 'What the hell are you talking about.'

'About the parting of the ways.' She made herself look at him, coolly and calmly. 'We had a deal, but today it ends. And nothing takes its place.'

There was a silence, then he said quietly, 'Darling, you don't—you can't mean that.' He unclipped her seat belt and reached for her.

She recoiled and said hoarsely, 'Don't touch me. Just—don't...'

'Oh, for God's sake.' His tone was harsh. 'I gave up wrestling in cars years ago. I just want to hold you while I find out what's going on here.'

'Haven't I made it clear enough?' she asked, her heart thudding. 'You hired me to do a job. My part of the bargain is complete. All that remains is for you, Mr Radley-Smith, to give me the money you promised.' She paused. 'Unless, of course, you consider that last night was payment in kind? All debts settled and nothing more due?'

'No,' he said, his eyes narrowing. 'I think nothing of the kind. And why this sudden ludicrous formality? You called out my first name when you were coming only a few hours ago.'

'That was then.' Marin kept her voice steady. 'This is now. So spare me any further reminders of last night's events, please.'

'Why should I do that?' Jake threw back at her. 'Or am I supposed to pretend it didn't happen?'

'Put it down to an error of judgement.' She hesitated. 'I shouldn't drink when I'm not used to it.'

'Oh no, darling,' he said softly. 'You can't blame the demon alcohol for that particular turn of events, and you know that as well as I do. We may not have been very wise, but we were both sober.' He paused. 'So—what's the real problem?'

'No problem at all.' She didn't look at him. 'I just have no wish to compound my mistake. And any further involvement with you, Mr Radley-Smith, would be a seriously bad idea.'

She swallowed. 'Or did you think, having given me the ultimate good time in bed, I'd be begging you for more?'

How could she be saying these things? she asked herself with a kind of anguish. Was this the price she had to pay for self-preservation? To ensure that he would leave her strictly alone from now on?

'That never crossed my mind,' he said. 'But I think I deserve some kind of explanation for this— *volte face*.'

'Of course,' she said. 'I'd almost forgotten. *You're* the one who usually decides when it's over and walks away. Well, this time it's my prerogative.'

'Is there someone else in your life?' he asked abruptly. 'Another man?'

'That's none of your business.' Marin lifted her chin. 'And you're not *in my life*, Mr Radley-Smith.

You just—passed through it.' She took another deep breath. 'And now maybe we could go back to London. Unless you'd prefer me to hitch a lift to the nearest station?'

'That won't be necessary.' His voice was as grim as his face. He buckled his seat belt and switched on the engine. 'Tell me one last thing, Marin. What actually became of the girl who slept in my arms last night?'

She shrugged. 'She woke up. It's that simple.'

'Really?' he asked ironically. 'I'll have to take your word for that. Because I find it incredibly complicated.' And he turned the car back on to the road and drove off with a burst of acceleration that she recognised as pure anger.

He'd assumed that she'd be happy to fall in with any plan he put to her, she thought, her throat tightening. And he didn't like to lose the initiative or be thwarted. It must have been a long time since he was the target of such positive resistance. Perhaps he wouldn't take his next lady so much for granted, she told herself, and wanted to burst into tears.

It was a long and silent journey. Marin sat, her fingers clasped so tightly in her lap that they ached, allowing herself an occasional surreptitious peep at his bleak profile.

She'd done what she had to, she told herself, even if she felt as if the heart had been torn out of her body in the process.

When they reached the flat, Jake slotted the car

into a parking place she'd have said was impossibly small. Always in control, she thought stonily.

As he lifted her bag from the boot, she held out her hand. 'I'll take that, please.'

He stared at her. 'May I not even come in with you?'

'No,' she said. 'Thank you.'

As she took the case from him, his fingers closed over hers.

'Marin,' he said. 'Not like this. Please. I know it's a cliché, but we really need to talk.'

'There's nothing left to say.' She moved a defensive shoulder. 'Your important client has been convinced that you're not after his wife. And that's what it was all about.'

'Apart from the money, of course,' he said.

'Of course,' Marin echoed. She turned away. 'You can mail me the cheque.'

'No,' he said. 'I prefer to deal with it now, even if we are in the street.'

He produced his cheque book, rested it on the roof of the car, wrote then tore out the slip and handed it to her.

She stared at the amount, then looked at him. 'It's not what we agreed,' she said. 'It's too much. Another thousand pounds too much.'

'Call it a bonus.' He shrugged, his blue gaze flicking over her. His sudden smile was reminiscent. Insolent. 'Let's say for services above and beyond the call of duty.' He paused. 'And I'll be in touch,' he added softly, then got back in the car and drove off.

Marin wanted to tear the cheque into tiny pieces and fling them after him, but something warned her that if she did, and he saw, he would know that it mattered to her—that it mattered terribly.

And that was something that needed to remain her secret for ever.

There was a note from Lynne waiting for her. 'At Mike's. Hope all went well. See you later,' it informed her succinctly.

No, it didn't, Marin thought. And, no, you won't.

She'd had time to think during those endless miles in the car, and to make a decision. She was due to travel down to Essex and the new assignment tomorrow, but there was nothing to stop her going that afternoon and spending the night in a bed and break-fast.

That way, she would not have to face her stepsister until she'd managed to regain some measure of control over her stormy emotions.

I can't tell her what really happened, she thought. I can't.

Jake's parting remark had set her alarm bells ringing too.

But if he can't find me he can't be in touch, she reassured herself.

She put the new travel-bag in the wardrobe just as it was and found her usual case, packing it efficiently and deftly with working gear, reverting to the crisp, businesslike person she'd lost sight of in a fit of momentary madness.

Then she sat down and composed a letter to
Lynne, keeping the tone deliberately upbeat as she
explained she was off to start her new job early and
would call on her mobile as soon as she was settled.
She did not, however, include the address of the
practice. What Lynne did not know, she could not
inadvertently pass on.

I need these four weeks, she thought, as a breathing space to put myself together again. And when I
come back I'll find somewhere else to live. Most of
the other girls at work share flats, and they often have
spare rooms. So I'll be all right. I'll be fine.

And, above all, for the next month I'll be too busy
to think. And perhaps because of this, please God, I
can start to forget him.

Didn't someone say he was easier to recover from
once you were out of bed? I can only pray that it's true.

'Rubbing shoulders with nature for the past month
doesn't seem to have done you much good,' was
Lynne's first comment once she'd hugged her.
'You're looking pale, my pet.'

Marin shrugged. 'They all took me out to the local
Chinese restaurant last night,' she returned. 'I think
the sweet and sour sauce seriously disagreed with
me. But I'm fine again now.'

Except that she wasn't, because Mike arrived that
evening, fresh from playing in a charity cricket-
match, and hefting a bulging carrier bag.

'To welcome home the exile,' he announced. 'I've

got all your favourites. Chow mein, Kung Po chicken, shrimps in special sauce, beef with water chestnuts and a paddy field of fried rice.'

This time, to Marin's dismay, just the smell did it, and she fled.

'If you're no better in the morning,' Lynne ordained sternly, handing her a glass of water, 'You must see the doctor. You could need antibiotics.'

'I'd settle for a stomach transplant,' Marin said wanly. 'I don't think I'll ever look a Chinese meal in the face again. Let's hope it's over.'

But she hoped in vain.

'Right,' Lynne said briskly, coming into the bedroom where she lay hunched and miserable under the covers. 'I've phoned Wendy Ingram and explained why you won't be in, and Dr Jarvis will see you at two-thirty.' She paused. 'Can I leave you anything? Hot coffee, maybe?'

Marin shuddered. 'I think I'll stick to water.'

But half an hour later, she felt a total fraud. 'I'll cancel that appointment and go to work,' she told herself with determination, putting on her robe and heading for the sitting room to use the phone.

She was checking the surgery number when she heard the hall door close, and assumed it was Lynne back to check up on her.

'Look,' she began. 'You're taking the mother-hen thing too far.'

'And you, sweetheart,' Jake said from the doorway, 'are getting your genders confused.'

Marin gasped, a hand flying to pull the edges of her robe closer. 'What—what do you want?'

He strolled forward, dark-suited, his silk tie loosened, his face cool, unreadable. 'You.'

Her heart lurched, but she faced him defiantly. 'I don't think so. Even you can't be that desperate for a woman.'

His brows lifted coldly. 'Just who are you insulting by that remark, sweetheart? Yourself or me?'

'I meant,' she said swiftly, 'that you must have better things to do elsewhere.'

'Possibly,' he said. 'But I didn't come here to make a pass at you and have it rejected.'

'Then why?'

'Because, before you vanished into the wilds of wherever, I told you we needed to talk.'

'And I made it clear that was unnecessary.'

'Also because Lynne told me you were ill,' he went on as if she hadn't spoken. 'And I was—concerned.'

'Then Lynne shouldn't have fussed,' she said. 'And as I'm quite all right again, you've no need to trouble yourself.'

'You don't think so?' He looked at her reflectively. 'Maybe you should cast your mind back a few weeks to our never-to-be-repeated night together. There could be a very different reason for your malaise.'

'What do you mean?'

'I mean, my sweet, that unless you were taking the

contraceptive pill you and I had unprotected sex—
more than once.' His mouth twisted wryly. 'Usually
I take my own precautions, but, as love-making was
never supposed to feature on the agenda that
weekend, I was completely unprepared. As I now
suspect you were too. So there could be—consequences.'

For a moment, she stared at him, her mind reeling.
Then she said huskily, 'No, it's not possible. I don't
believe it.'

'Then let's see if your faith is justified,' he said.
He took a flat packet from his inside pocket and
tossed it to her. 'Pop into the bathroom, if you will,
and put both our minds at rest.'

Marin stared down at the pregnancy-testing kit,
her heart beating like a drum in sheer panic. 'No,'
she said. 'No—I can't.'

'Why not? The instructions seem perfectly clear.
And I certainly can't do it for you.'

'All right, then, I won't.' She lifted her chin. 'You
have no right to march in here, giving me orders.'

'I wish to know whether or not you're carrying my
child,' he said. 'I'd say that's well within my rights.
So, please do as I ask. For both our sakes.'

Their eyes met, clashed. Then Marin turned and
stalked off to the bathroom.

She could simply throw the kit away when she
was alone, she thought, and tell him the result was
negative. That he could leave with a clear con-
science.

Except that she needed to allay the sudden terrifying doubt in her own mind. Reassure herself that the frantic mental sums she'd already been doing were all wrong that her period was often late, and that she really was fine, with nothing to fear.

Above all she needed to watch him walk away and know that she would never have to experience the hurt of seeing him again.

Peace of mind, she told herself, in a little box.

When she finally returned to the living room, Jake needed to take only one look at her white face and quivering lips. He was silent for a moment, then sighed.

'That settles it,' he said. 'Now we really do have to talk.' As he walked towards her, she took a step back and saw his mouth tighten. He took her hand and led her to the sofa.

She tried to free herself. 'Leave me alone.'

'Don't be silly.' His voice was quite gentle as he drew her down beside him. 'Sit down before you fall down.' He paused. 'I suppose our first priority is to tell your mother and stepfather. Find out how soon they can get here.'

She stared at him, mute with horror at all the additional implications of this discovery. The thought of having to tell Barbara and Derek what a total mess she'd made of her life—to inflict such a terrible disappointment—made her cringe inside.

Confessing to Lynne would be just as bad, but she knew her stepsister would help her, get her through whatever needed to be done. She felt sick all over again at the prospect.

She said, stumbling over the words. 'I'd rather not—tell them.'

'I'm sure,' he said drily. 'I'm not looking forward to telling my mother, either. But it has to be done.' He paused. 'It will have to be a special licence, and the local registrar, of course, and we need to set the date as soon as possible.'

The words swam in her head, making no sense. No sense at all.

She stared at him, 'Please—what are you talking about?' she whispered.

'About our wedding, naturally,' he said with a touch of impatience. 'We're having a baby, Marin, so we're going to get married. And that's all there is to it.'

'But you're not the marrying kind.' Her protest was instant and unthinking.

'Perhaps not,' he agreed. 'And I certainly had no plans for fatherhood, either. How quickly life can change.'

'Oh, for God's sake.' She made a little half-helpless, half-impatient gesture. 'No one has to get married these days—not for this kind of reason.'

'Then I must be curiously old-fashioned,' Jake said icily. 'Because I have no intention of allowing my firstborn to be a bastard.'

My firstborn…

Oh God, she thought, wanting to cry. Oh, God.

She didn't look at him. Her voice was a stranger's.

'You're overlooking the alternative. There—there doesn't have to be a baby at all.'

'I'm overlooking nothing,' he returned shortly. 'And you're not going down that path, Marin, not even if I have to chain you to my wrist until it's too late. Whatever they may say, it's not an easy option. And we're not taking the risk.'

'But we can't be married, either.' She felt herself shrinking into her corner of the sofa. 'We—we hardly know each other.'

'Not in terms of weeks, months or years, perhaps,' he agreed. His mouth twisted ruefully. 'But in one important area we've proved we're entirely compatible, if a little careless.'

'I told you—I'd been drinking. I—I didn't realise what I was doing.'

'Well, you're sober now,' he said softly. He slipped off his jacket, threw it over the arm of the sofa. Undid his tie. 'Why don't we adjourn to the bedroom and put your interesting theory to the test?'

'No!' The word choked out of her. 'Don't you dare touch me.'

His brows drew together. 'As I remarked just now, how quickly life can change,' he said, half to himself. 'I must ask Graham where he gets his booze. It must be amazing stuff to have managed to overcome, even for a few hours, your aversion to me.'

'So I made a terrible mistake,' she went on hoarsely, ignoring his loaded comment. 'That's no reason to wreck the rest of my life.'

He was silent for a moment. 'No,' he said at last. 'And for that I'm more sorry than you can imagine. I should, of course, have taken more care of you. Protected you from any consequences. I blame myself entirely.'

He sighed abruptly. 'But at least I can guarantee that your future sufferings will be endured in a reasonable degree of comfort.'

'Am I supposed to find that reassuring?' she asked bitterly.

He shrugged. 'What else can I tell you? I'm healthy. I don't smoke, don't do drugs, and have never, in spite of some intense provocation, lifted my hand to a woman. Nor,' he added deliberately, 'do I drink to excess.'

She flushed angrily. 'And that's supposed to be sufficient basis for marriage?'

He was leaning back, totally at ease, long legs stretched out in front of him. 'It's a beginning,' he said. 'I imagine you don't require me to go down on one knee and express my undying devotion.'

'No,' Marin said stonily. 'I see no need for unnecessary lies.'

'But there may be times when you won't want the unvarnished truth from me, either.' His gaze was sardonic. 'Therefore, can I be sure that you won't probe too deeply if I tell you I'm working late?'

'No.' Her throat felt as if a hand had closed round it, crushing the life from her. 'Although it could make life difficult for Lynne, if she has to back up your story.'

He said flatly, 'Lynne will no longer be working for me.'

Marin shot out of her corner. 'You mean, you're firing her?' she demanded hotly. 'God, that's so unfair. This isn't her fault.'

'Oh, calm down,' Jake said wearily. 'I'm promoting her to associate director. It includes a salary raise, and a much better benefits package all round. It's been on the cards for a while, and she thoroughly deserves it, but she'll be bloody hard to replace. So you're not the only loser in all this, my sweet.'

'Don't call me that!'

'What would you prefer?' he enquired mockingly. 'My darling? My one and only love?'

She sank back against the cushions again. 'Please,' she said quietly. 'Please—don't.'

'Then I'll stick to Marin,' he said. 'On one condition—that from now on you call me Jake.' He added almost casually. 'You can start practising this afternoon when you meet my mother.'

She stared at him. 'You have a mother?'

'Of course,' he returned. 'How did you imagine I got here? I think the pair of us have exploded the stork myth pretty thoroughly.'

She said defensively, 'I didn't realise you had any relatives.'

'I also have three godparents, two aunts, an uncle, plus their spouses and various cousins.' He paused. 'But I suggest we restrict the wedding to immediate family only.'

She looked down at her hands clenched tightly in her lap. 'Surely there's some arrangement other than marriage we could reach—if you really want to acknowledge you're the baby's father?'

'Ah,' he said. 'Agreed access in return for child support, I suppose?' He spoke with a kind of cool implacability. 'I'm afraid I'm not prepared to settle for a couple of hours every fortnight, depending on your convenience. I've watched it happen in the lives of people I know, and it hasn't been pretty.'

His eyes met hers. 'My child will have a stable home and be cared for by both its parents. Because the baby's welfare is all that matters, and our personal feelings have to take second place.'

'And what happens when the baby's old enough to realise he's the only reason that his parents are together?' Her mouth was dry—so dry. 'That—that they don't love each other?'

Jake shrugged. 'We cross that bridge when we come to it. Or we go back to square one and pretend like crazy.'

'Beginning with your mother, I suppose?' Marin bit her lip.

'No,' he said. 'I intend to tell her the truth. She moved out of the Manor to a house on the edge of the village when Dad died three years ago, but she looks after things on the estate for me and acts as my hostess when necessary, so we see a lot of each other.' He paused, adding flatly, 'And she's not easy to fool.'

Manor? Marin thought, startled. Estate? That didn't sound like the weekend glamour-pad for entertaining his girlfriends that she'd imagined. On the contrary, it held new and even more disturbing implications which she would have to consider later. When she was alone.

She said unevenly, 'And my mother—my stepfather—what do I say to them?'

'Tell them what seems best,' he said. 'But they could find the situation easier to accept if you were able to convince them that ours was a love match instead of a case of *force majeure*.

'And you might try that same approach to Sadie,' he added. 'She's now the housekeeper at the Manor, but she used to be my nanny, and she doesn't mince her words when she decides I've overstepped the mark. However, she has a romantic soul, and might be slightly mollified if she thought we'd been carried away by our mutual passion—even though it won't spare me the tongue-lashing of the century.'

'And for how long would I be expected to maintain this farce?' Marin felt as if she was dying inside but she managed a flash of her old spirit.

'I'd say until I allow my obvious and unforgivable failings as a husband to destroy the glow of married bliss,' he said cynically. 'I won't make you wait too long.' He gave her a level look. 'So, do I take it my honourable proposal has been accepted? For the baby's sake?'

She was silent for a moment, then she said very

quietly, 'Yes—for the baby. But for no other reason. I want to make that totally clear.'

He shrugged. 'As daylight.'

'But I can't meet your mother today,' she went on. 'I have a doctor's appointment at two-thirty.'

'Then I'll go with you,' he said pleasantly. 'And we can drive down to the country afterwards and face Mother together.'

He glanced at his watch and rose, picking up his jacket and tie. 'Now, I must get back to the office.' He paused. 'Do you want me to say anything to Lynne?'

'No,' she said quickly. 'Oh God, no.'

He nodded. 'Then I'll leave it to you. But please don't let it slip your mind,' he added evenly. 'And when I come back at two to collect you, Marin, make sure you're here.'

'Yes,' she said. 'I will be.' Her smile hurt. 'After all, what real choice do I have?'

'None,' Jake said harshly. 'But, in case you've forgotten, that applies to us both.'

She was aware of him crossing the room. His footsteps in the hall. The outer door closing.

Then and only then, as silence closed in on her and she could be quite sure she was alone, she buried her face in her hands and stayed without moving, crouched in her corner of the sofa, for a very long time.

CHAPTER TEN

'WHY DID YOU cancel your medical appointment?'
Jake asked as they drove out of London that afternoon.

'It seemed pointless to ask the doctor about food
poisoning when I knew the real diagnosis.' Marin
didn't mention that she had done a second test in
case, by some miracle the first result had been wrong.
Nor did she tell him that, at that point, she'd cried
until she had no tears left as she contemplated the
bleak future awaiting her as Jake's unwanted wife
and mother of his only child.

Eventually, she'd regained a measure of composure and had done something about her appearance
too. She'd been appalled when she'd looked in the
bedroom mirror and saw herself as he must have
done—the pale, drawn face, the lank hair and elderly
dressing-gown.

I'm amazed he didn't run out screaming, she
thought wanly.

But then her lack of physical attraction no longer
mattered. Not when he'd made it clear his sole

concern was the tiny life they'd unintentionally created together.

So she showered, washed her hair, then dressed in a pale blue denim skirt, and a sleeveless white top. She made discreet use of concealer and blusher to disguise her pallor.

Now if only they'd invent a cosmetic called 'happy', she thought, it would make pretending much easier.

She'd also heated some soup and managed to keep a whole bowlful down, which was quite an achievement, considering the state of nervous tension she was under.

'Well, it doesn't really matter. When you get to Chelsea you'll be seeing my doctor, anyway,' Jake said, frowning. 'I'll call him tomorrow.'

'Isn't that a little soon?' she asked tautly.

'No.' He sent her an unsmiling glance. 'Because you're moving in with me tonight.'

There was a silence, then Marin said unevenly, 'Please don't make me do this. I'm fine where I am with Lynne.'

'And I prefer you to be under my roof where I can keep an eye on you.' He added flatly, 'Anyway, Lynne won't be staying at the flat much longer. She and Mike have found their own place, and it's ready to move into.'

'They didn't tell me.' Only a month, she thought, but everything was changing, the ground shifting under her feet.

'They were probably waiting until you felt better.'

'Presumably you don't feel the same need to be considerate.'

'It's hardly inconsiderate to want to take care of you,' Jake retorted. 'And, as we're going to be married, living with me beforehand is no big deal.' He added drily, 'Lynne and Mike certainly don't think so, anyway.'

She thought with swift desolation, 'But they love each other…'

Aloud, she said, 'When you say—I'll be living with you…?'

'Ah,' he said softly. 'Can we be back to the vexed question of sleeping arrangements once again?'

'Yes,' Marin said baldly. 'Please understand I want my own room. Before and after the wedding. Not conditional.'

There was a sudden tension in the car, flowing between them like an electric current.

But when Jake spoke he sounded relaxed, even faintly amused. 'Now, how did I know you were going to say that?' he asked. 'Don't worry, Marin. I've already given the appropriate instructions.' His mouth twisted wryly. 'Although, as we both know, separate rooms is hardly any guarantee of good behaviour.'

Marin felt the colour rising in her face. 'On the contrary.' She kept her voice steady. 'I have no intention of making the same mistake twice.'

'Nor have I, darling,' Jake said softly. 'Nor have I.'

She decided it would be wise to change the subject. 'Did—did you speak to your mother?'

'Yes,' he said after a pause. 'We had a fairly frank discussion.'

'Is she very angry?'

'She's certainly disappointed,' he returned. 'But she appears to have accepted the situation.'

'Lucky you,' Marin said bitterly. 'I suspect my mother will react rather differently to the news.'

'Just as well we're not having the banns called,' he said pleasantly. 'She might have forbidden them.'

'This is not some kind of joke,' she flared.

'No,' he said tersely. 'It's not. And I've never felt less like laughing in my life. But we have to get through this, Marin, so weeping, wailing and teeth-gnashing will do no good, either.' He paused. 'Agreed?'

She looked down at her hands, gripped together in her lap, and nodded silently.

She was never to forget her first glimpse of Harborne Manor.

She'd half-expected something formal and Georgian, on the lines of Queens Barton, not this graceful mass of grey stone topped by tall, eccentric chimneys, its age enhanced by its mullioned windows and wide-arched entrance, which seemed to lift itself from the surrounding grassland as they approached.

She leaned forward. 'My God.' Her voice was stunned. 'It's beautiful. I never dreamed...' She swallowed. 'Is it open to the public?'

'No, it's not,' Jake returned. 'It is and always will be

a private house. Although, we allow visitors in to our Garden Day in June to raise money for the Red Cross.'

'Garden Day?' Marin repeated in a hollow tone, and saw his mouth relax into something like genuine amusement.

'Don't worry,' he said. 'It was held three weeks ago. Anyway, you're not short of organisational skills in your career.'

But not quite to this extent, Marin thought, swallowing.

As he brought the car to a halt on the gravelled sweep in front of the main entrance, a woman emerged and stood on the steps, waiting for them.

She was large, with a round, rosy face, her grey silver-streaked hair drawn back from her face into a loose knot.

'Well, here she is, Sadie,' Jake called as they approached the steps. 'She didn't escape while she had the chance.'

Marin found herself being swept by a lightning scrutiny from unexpectedly shrewd brown eyes.

'And why should the young lady do any such thing, Mr James? Now, enough nonsense and introduce us properly.'

'Yes, ma'am,' Jake murmured, grinning.

His task performed, Marin was subjected to another head-to-toe assessment.

'Too thin by far,' was Sadie Hubbard's brisk verdict. 'And not feeling too clever, either, I dare say. Nasty thing, morning sickness, but it soon passes, thank the Lord.' She turned a steely look on her former charge. 'But no thanks to you, Mr James.'

'No, Sadie,' Jake agreed with suspicious meekness. Taking Marin's hand before she could move out of range, he drew her towards him and dropped a kiss on her hair. 'This is your home, darling,' he told her softly. 'Come and have a look at it.'

She remembered him touching her hair, lifting it away so he could brush the nape of her neck with his mouth, and everything that had followed.

It didn't mean a thing to him, she thought with pain. It was the kind of casual caress he must have bestowed a hundred times. He could never have expected her to react as she had done. And she had to live with the shame of that.

And, like he was doing now, pretend.

By some supreme effort she made herself look at him, smile, leave her hand in his light clasp and let him lead her indoors.

Where she stopped dead, her breath catching when she saw the size of the panelled hall and the magnificently carved oak staircase with its galleried landing.

'How old is all this?' she whispered as she looked wonderingly around her.

'Originally it was Tudor,' Jake said. 'Probably built from the stones of some unfortunate monastery. But it's been altered and added to a great deal since then—mostly in the days before listed buildings and planning departments. Fortunately my father and grandfather confined themselves merely to sorting out the plumbing,' he added. 'So you won't have to break the ice on the well if you want a bath.'

'As if anyone ever did,' Sadie snorted. 'Now, behave yourself, Mr James, and take Miss Wade out to your mother on the terrace before she really does run away.'

'So this is Marin.' Elizabeth Radley-Smith was a tall woman, dark-haired and calm-faced. Her eyes were vivid blue, like Jake's, but there was no gleam of laughter in their depths. Her expression was concerned, even wary, and she offered no other welcome than a brief handshake.

She may have accepted the situation, thought Marin bleakly as she accepted a seat in the trellised arbour, shady with fragrant honeysuckle, where a wooden table and cushioned wicker-chairs had been placed. But she doesn't have to like it, or me. And who can blame her?

'I'm going to speak to Cook about tea,' Mrs Radley-Smith said after an awkward pause. 'Why don't you talk to Marin about what we discussed earlier?'

'What does your mother want to suggest?' Marin asked tautly as the older woman departed. 'That I make myself scarce for the next eight months, then have the baby adopted?'

Jake's mouth tightened. 'On the contrary. She rang

me back to ask if we'd be prepared to forego the civil ceremony in town and be married here, by special licence, in the parish church. She reckons we could have an equally quiet wedding if we picked some mid-week morning and had a celebration family lunch here afterwards.'

She stared at him. 'You—you want to be married in church?'

'Why not?' Jake retorted. 'I was christened and confirmed there, and I sometimes go with Ma to Evensong when I'm down for the weekend. I've even been known to read the lesson on occasion. And could you stop looking at me as if I'd grown a second head?' he added with faint asperity.

'I'm sorry.' Marin shook her head. 'I find all this rather difficult to reconcile with your lifestyle.'

He said levelly, 'I do what's expected of me, Marin, as you have reason to know.' He paused. 'But what do you feel about Ma's suggestion? It has the added bonus that all your family could stay at the Manor before during and after the wedding, if they wished. Give me a chance to get to know them.'

She stared at him, the words, 'I do what's expected of me' still echoing in her mind. 'I don't know what to say.' She hesitated. 'I presume you wouldn't expect me to be married in white?'

'Wear a bin bag if you want,' Jake said brusquely. 'Just be there. I'll speak to the vicar, fix up a suitable day.'

'Won't this hasty marriage spoil your "pillar of the community" image?'

His mouth twisted. 'Why should it? I'm not planning to book the christening at the same time. Anyway, Mr Arnold is one of the least judgmental men I know.'

Mrs Radley-Smith appeared, carrying a tray, which Jake leapt up and took from her. 'Jake and I are having builders' tea,' she announced. 'But I've asked Cook to make you a special peppermint infusion, Marin. Jake tells me you're having sickness problems, and I found it helped me a lot when I was first pregnant.'

Marin bit her lip. 'Thank you. That's very kind.'

Or maybe, she thought, she doesn't want me throwing up all over these old and probably irreplaceable flagstones.

Mrs Radley-Smith sat down. 'So, have you come to any decision about the wedding?'

'I'm still trying to persuade her.' Jake smiled at Marin as she took her cup of peppermint tea.

'I do hope you agree,' Mrs Radley-Smith went on rather stiffly. 'It's a very beautiful old church, and generations of our family have been married there. I feel the local people, and the vicar particularly, would be most disappointed if Jake chose to have his wedding somewhere else. Also, Mr Arnold prefers to use the old prayer-book service, which I also favour.'

Marin stared down into her cup. Phrases like 'to

love and to cherish' and 'till death do us part' were whirling in her head suddenly. Jake, she thought, would stand beside her and say these things, and she would have to respond and pretend she believed him. Pretend that their marriage was going to be a real one instead of a convenient sham.

With my body, I thee worship...

And she, *she,* would have to pretend she didn't care. That she wasn't longing—aching for him.

Pain slashed her. She thought. 'I can't do this. I can't be such a hypocrite.' And only realised she'd spoken aloud when she heard Mrs Radley-Smith's sharp intake of breath and saw Jake's mouth tighten grimly.

He said, 'Then a civil ceremony in London it shall be. And that's final.'

It was not the easiest meal Marin had ever sat through. Jake and his mother chatted in a desultory way about local matters while she made herself drink her tea and nibble a slice of wholemeal bread and butter with some local honey. But she knew her decision over the wedding rankled.

Eventually, Jake pushed back his chair and rose. 'I need to phone the office. I'll tell Sadie to begin the guided tour without me.'

Marin was torn between relief and an overwhelming urge to grab the front of his shirt and beg, 'Don't leave me.'

But that, she thought, would be tantamount to a declaration of love, and hideously embarrassing for both of them.

Left alone, the two women sat in silence for a few moments, then Marin said with difficulty, 'You must really hate me.'

'I don't hate anybody,' said Mrs Radley-Smith. 'With the exception of people who abuse children or animals, and I'm sure you don't fall into either category.'

'But you can't want Jake to be married—like this.'

'No, I don't. Far from it.'

'Then couldn't you talk to him before it's too late?' Marin begged unhappily. 'Persuade him, somehow, it's a bad idea and that there must be a better solution?'

The older woman shook her head. 'As well try and stop a herd of charging elephants than Jake with his mind made up. And he wants his child born in wedlock. So it seems as if we all have to make the best of things.'

She gave Marin a level look. 'But I love my son, Miss Wade, and what grieves me most about this whole unfortunate business is that you'd apparently prefer to be a single mother rather than become his wife.'

She paused. 'However, as you must have realised by now, Harborne Manor is very old and very beautiful, and I found it a more than happy home,' she added with a catch in her voice. 'Perhaps when you've seen round it, you may become more reconciled to your changed circumstances.'

Marin lifted her chin. 'You think that makes a difference? That maybe I see the baby as a stepping stone to a life of luxury with a rich man footing my bills? Because I promise you I don't. I knew that Jake had a home in the country, because my sister, who works for him, mentioned it, but I didn't realise its scale, or what was involved.'

'Well, no,' said Mrs Radley-Smith. 'But then the kind of relationship you had with my son—a one-night stand, I believe it's called—hardly invites confidences of that nature. Does it?'

There was a loaded silence, then Marin said quietly, 'Please believe, Mrs Radley-Smith, that I cannot feel any more ashamed about what occurred than I already do.'

The older woman sighed abruptly. 'And I'm ashamed too,' she said. 'I swore I wouldn't do this. That I'd already said all that was necessary to my son. But it's just that Jake is so very dear to me—and I'd hoped so much...'

As her voice incredibly faltered, Marin intervened hurriedly, 'I'm sorry too—for everything.' She shook her head. 'But—twenty-four hours ago I thought I knew where my life was going. Now, it's been—turned upside down. And I'm not coping very well.'

'But you must have realised the risk you'd taken?' Mrs Radley-Smith had herself in hand again, the blue eyes coolly questioning.

'I went straight into a pretty demanding job,' Marin said. 'My mind got taken up with other things.'

Like trying not to be in love with Jake. Wanting to forget everything about that night in his arms. Coming to terms with a future that he would never be a part of.

And, in that last respect at least, nothing had changed. Except that now she would even be denied the mercy of never seeing him again, of finding some way to heal her heartache and start her life afresh without him.

And sleeping in another bed, another room, apart from him would be like trying to staunch a severed artery with a sticking plaster. Especially when he'd made it clear he would not be spending his own nights at home, or alone.

How can I bear this? she asked herself desperately. How can I bear any of it?

Mrs Radley-Smith gave a faint sigh, then pushed back her chair and rose. 'Well, you'll soon have an even more demanding occupation,' she said. 'When you become a wife and mother. And now I'll take you to Sadie.'

'A wife and mother,' Marin repeated silently under her breath as she followed Elizabeth into the house.

She knew that the only real hope left to her was her ability to survive the rest of the day without betraying even for a second that she was weeping inside.

Thankfully, Sadie showed no inclination to begin the interrogation that Marin was dreading. She merely conducted her round the Manor with a pride that was almost tangible.

And with every reason, Marin admitted as she gazed around her. The downstairs rooms were spacious in spite of their low ceilings, and furnished with an emphasis on comfort rather than display, each with its own stone fireplace filled now with attractive arrangements of dried flowers for the summer. The ancient wooden floors were laid with Persian rugs, and almost every gleaming surface held a bowl of scented roses or *pot pourri* to mingle with the aroma of wax polish.

Beyond the deep, low windows, Marin glimpsed splashes of brilliant colour in the flower gardens at the rear of the house.

'And we grow nearly all our own vegetables too,' Sadie told her. 'Mr Murtric is very keen on the organics.'

Mr Murtrie, Marin reminded herself as she murmured an appreciative response, was the head gardener with two trainees to help him. The cook was Mrs Osborne; her daughter, Cherry, did the housework, with assistance from the village, and was married to Bob Fielding, who looked after the horses.

I should have brought a notebook, she thought grimly, and written it all down together with a family tree. Plus a map of the layout. Otherwise, I'm never going to remember any of it.

It occurred to her too that she was apparently carrying the heir to a dynasty of several hundred years, and this had to be why Jake was so insis-

tent on marriage. He wants a son, she thought.
Not a wife.

Yet for all that, and almost in spite of herself, she
was beginning to relax, to feel a kind of peace
stealing over her. As if, she realised with bewilderment, the house was reaching out to her, wrapping
her in warmth and security.

Which was, of course, absurd. She was here,
stupidly and quite unforgivably, because of an accident
of nature. She would always be the outsider—the in-
terloper—and anything else was fantasy.

Remember that, she advised herself grimly. And
don't let yourself hope—even for a moment—that
your life could be different.

Because Diana Halsay's contemptuous analogy
of the starving kid looking in the baker's window
was proving horribly accurate.

One of the rooms she liked best was rather smaller
than the others, and shabbily cosy.

'It used to be called the Ladies' Parlour,' said
Sadie. 'Because it's where they used to sit and do
their sewing in the old days. But it's more a family
room now.' She added, 'When Mr James comes
down at weekends, he likes to sit here in the evenings
to play his music and read.'

Marin, on the point of asking how many of his
weekends Jake spent at the Manor, stopped herself
just in time, realising this was information she was
supposed to know already.

But it appeared there were often times when Jake

stopped being the womanising workaholic of London legend, she thought ruefully. In fact, 'Mr James' was becoming more of a surprise package with every minute that passed.

She said, 'If his name is James, why is he known as Jake?'

'His grandfather wanted him christened Jacob, which is a family name,' Sadie explained. 'But Madam didn't care for it, so she and her husband, Mr Philip, compromised on James. But the old gentleman, who always liked to get his own way, started calling him Jake, and it stuck.' She added firmly, 'However, I believe in baptismal names, so he's always Mr James to me.'

And Jake to me, thought Marin as they started up the broad staircase, and clearly a chip off his grandfather's block in his determination to obtain his own way. Or I would not be here.

'Mr James suggested we should start with the master suite,' Sadie went on, leading the way along the gallery. 'He thought you might have some ideas about a change of decor.'

Marin hung back, her face warming. 'I'm sure it's all fine,' she said. 'I'd really rather not intrude on his privacy.'

Sadie gave her an indulgent if surprised glance. 'Bless you, Mr James still sleeps in his old room. The master suite hasn't been used since Mr Philip died and Madam moved down to the village, so it's due for a bit of refurbishment. It will make a nice project for you both,' she added, nodding.

And keep you out of mischief...

She didn't have to say the words aloud; they were there, hovering in the air, Marin thought, biting her lip as she reluctantly followed Sadie into the room.

Her first thought was that it was like walking into sunlight, an impression enhanced by the gold brocade draperies at the windows, and the matching quilted coverlet on the wide bed.

She said softly, 'Oh, how lovely.'

'That's as maybe, but I knew these curtains would fade.' Sadie examined them, tutting with disapproval. 'I told Madam so, but she only laughed and said that Mr Philip liked them, which was all that mattered.' She sighed. 'It was wrong for him to be taken from her like that, and them so devoted.'

'What happened?' Marin asked.

'He'd been out looking at some new fruit trees that had just been planted, and he came in complaining of a bad headache. He took a couple of painkillers and said he'd lie down on the couch in his study for a little while. When Madam went to call him for tea, she found him unconscious, and he died on the way to hospital.' She sighed again. 'The doctors said it was a cerebral aneurism.'

Marin said huskily, 'My father's death was terribly sudden too, but in his case it was a heart attack.'

Sadie patted her arm. 'It's a hard thing for those

left behind,' she said gently. 'But Madam has done her grieving, and now it's time for some happiness to return to the house—with a new generation.'

She became practical again. 'Now, that door over there is the bathroom, and next to it is the dressing room. So why don't you have a look round on your own for a few minutes, see what you think?'

I think, Marin said under her breath, that I seem to be taking part in my own personal disaster movie, and I haven't learned my lines yet.

She smiled and murmured something acquiescent. She tried not to look at the big, golden bed as she crossed first to the bathroom—its azure tiles setting off the big white tub, the separate shower cubicle and the twin basins—then walked into the adjoining dressing-room and went in, standing to stare around at its range of fitted wardrobes, cupboards and sets of drawers. And its single bed.

'Enjoying the tour?' Jake asked as she walked into the bedroom. He was lounging across the bed, propped up on one elbow, his smile crooked as he looked at her.

'It's—interesting.' She glanced round the room, trying to avoid the memories that the casual positioning of his lean body seemed to be relentlessly evoking. Reminding her of him reaching for her, pulling her towards him. Under him.

She added, dry-mouthed, 'Where's Mrs Hubbard— Sadie?'

'Don't panic,' he advised coolly. 'She's not far

away. And I told you she was romantic at heart. So she's left us alone in the bedroom she believes we'll be sharing to allow us to contemplate the imminent joys of legalised sex.' His tone bit. 'I decided not to destroy her illusions quite yet.'

He paused. 'What did you think of the doghouse?'

'I don't understand.'

'My father's name for the dressing room,' Jake explained. 'He said it used to be a place of exile for husbands who'd committed some sin or were simply surplus to requirements.' He paused. 'As I seem to fit both descriptions, I'd better prepare to move in—at the same time scoring points for being so considerate about my bride's delicate state,' he added silkily.

Marin's face warmed, but she lifted her chin. 'Actually, I plan to sleep there myself.'

'I don't think so.' Jake shook his head. 'In a few months you're going to find a single bed rather less than comfortable. And I shall only be here at weekends, anyway, so what the hell?'

Marin said sharply, 'Don't you mean—*we* will be here?'

'No,' Jake said coolly. 'I do not. After the wedding, you'll be based down here, not London.'

Her voice shook. 'You think I'm going to be left here—alone?'

His brows lifted. 'It's hardly solitary confinement. You'll be well taken care of. Even cherished.'

'I'm not an invalid,' she said stormily. 'And I have

a job I like and wish to continue. I do not plan to become—a vegetable.'

'What were you thinking of?' he enquired with polite interest. 'A Jerusalem artichoke, perhaps, or a cauliflower?'

'Don't you dare laugh about this.' Her eyes blazed at him. 'It's my whole life I'm talking about.'

Jake swung himself lithely off the bed and took a step towards her. Marin gasped and took a corresponding step backwards, a move that again was not lost on him.

He halted, his mouth hardening. He said crisply, 'Your life has changed, sweetheart, and so has your job description. You're about to become my wife, and I prefer not to have you disappearing in your condition to God knows where and for weeks on end.

'However,' he went on. 'I also get the distinct impression that the less we see of each other the better. Or am I wrong?'

'No.' She stared down at the gleaming floorboards. 'You're not wrong. So couldn't we at least reconsider my moving to Chelsea?'

'Nice try, darling, but the arrangement stands.' His smile was pure winter. 'We have a busy time ahead of us. Even the simplest wedding takes a measure of organisation, and this will be more conveniently achieved if we're under the same roof. But I'll make sure that our togetherness is kept to a minimum. Console yourself with that.'

'And how do you plan to console your mother?'

Marin asked tautly. 'How is she going to feel seeing someone like me living here, trying to take her place?'

'Firstly, you'll be creating your own place,' Jake said quietly. 'Not filling someone else's shoes.

'Secondly, I think Ma's concerns are rather different.' He paused. 'She and my father were very much in love, and she's always hoped that when I married it would be for the same reason.'

'Then why didn't you do that?' She flung back her head. 'You must have had enough adoring women hanging round you.'

'Ah,' he said. 'But the adoration has to be mutual. You see the problem?'

She said in a stifled voice, 'Yes, I see it.'

'Then consider this too,' he said. 'As it's supremely obvious that you and I have been on terms of intimacy at some point, maybe you could stop reeling back in alarm each time I approach you. Unless, of course, you wish to give the impression that I raped you.'

She looked at him, her eyes stricken. 'No,' she got out. 'You can't possibly think—'

'I'm trying very hard not to think at all,' he cut across her abruptly. 'Not with any great success. But the fact remains that there are going to be times when we shall have to touch each other, however reluctantly. Beginning with this unavoidable formality.' He reached into his shirt pocket and produced something that danced and glittered in the sunlight.

He said, 'Give me your hand.' Then sighed. 'Marin—your left hand, please.'

She looked down speechlessly at the ring he was putting on her finger. At the exquisite pigeon's-blood ruby flanked by the pure brilliance of diamonds.

At last, she said unevenly, 'I can't possibly accept this. It's not right.'

'It was my grandmother's ring,' he said. 'Left to me for precisely this moment.'

'But not this girl.' The look she sent him was almost desperate. 'I'd be wearing it under false pretences.'

'There's no pretence,' Jake told her. 'You are now officially my fiancée. Very shortly you'll become my wife. To the outside world, we're lovers, and the rings you wear will demonstrate this.'

He was still clasping her hand, Marin realised, looking down at the blaze of the gemstones as if they mesmerised him. The room seemed oddly hushed, and for one aching moment as they stood, enclosed in sunlight, she thought he was going to lift her fingers to his lips. She knew that she should not—must not—allow this...

Then the door opened and Sadie came bustling in. 'Madam's waiting to say goodbye,' she announced. 'She has a meeting this evening—the village-hall committee.'

Jake released Marin's hand and stepped back.

'We should go too,' he said. 'We have things to do

in London.' He looked at her, his blue gaze compelling. 'Don't we, darling?'

And she heard herself whisper, 'Yes.'

CHAPTER ELEVEN

'I'D LIKE TO murder him,' Lynne said furiously. 'Oh God, he promised me—he swore that he'd look after you—that you'd be safe with him.'

Marin said in a low voice, 'It wasn't his fault.'

Lynne's lips parted in a soundless gasp. She said, 'You mean you went with someone else? Oh, Marin, not that bastard in France. Surely not…?'

'No,' Marin said wretchedly. 'It's Jake's baby.' She shook her head. 'But I'm to blame, not him.'

'Now you're being ridiculous,' Lynne said robustly. 'After all, you didn't grab him and drag him into bed.' There was a long silence, and she went on more slowly, 'Marin—say something. You're beginning to worry me.'

'But that's exactly what I did,' Marin swallowed. 'Lynne, I was hardly wearing any clothes and I—I threw myself at him.'

'Dear God,' Lynne said blankly. She got to her feet. 'I need some strong coffee. Do you want some?'

'I've changed to peppermint tea. There's a packet

in the kitchen.' A present from my future mother-in-law, she thought, biting her lip.

Lynne's face was brooding when she returned with the drinks. 'I don't understand any of this,' she said. 'For God's sake, Marin, you're the last person on earth to do something like that. So why, honey? And with Rad, of all people?'

Which was, of course, the fifty-million-dollar question, and Marin couldn't answer it. At least, not truthfully.

'I suppose I wanted to know what it was like,' she said eventually, looking away and praying that it sounded plausible. 'And with someone who'd know what he was doing.'

'A baby,' Lynne said quietly, 'is a high price to pay for curiosity.'

She drank some of her coffee. 'Is he going to admit he's the father? Provide financial support?'

'Yes,' Marin said. 'But not quite in the way you think.' She took her hand from its hiding place in her skirt pocket and held it out. 'We—we're getting married. He took me down to Harborne—to his house in the country—to meet his mother this afternoon. And he inherited this ring from his grandmother.'

Another silence, then Lynne sighed again, very wearily. 'I think in my secret heart I was praying this was some kind of weird wind-up,' she said. 'That you'd suddenly shout "April Fool", and I could kick you on the ankle for giving me a fright whereupon life would return to normal. Only it isn't going to—is it?'

She took Marin's cold hand in both of hers. 'And you say you're not in love with each other?'

'Not in the slightest.' Marin met her searching look calmly. 'We're making the best of a bad job, that's all. Jake doesn't want to be married in any conventional sense, but he needs an heir. I've no wish to be his wife in any sense at all, but I'm having his child.' She made herself shrug. 'Deal done. Problem solved.'

'Solved?' Lynne repeated incredulously. 'It sounds like a recipe for hell. Have you gone quite crazy?'

'No,' Marin said quietly. 'The madness was getting pregnant in the first place. But all that matters from now on is ensuring the baby has the best possible life.' *I have to believe that. Have to...*

'And your life?' Lynne asked. 'What about that?'

'Once the baby's born, I plan to go back to work in some capacity.'

'That's not what I meant,' Lynne said quietly. 'And you know it. Are you really going to be content with this sterile bargain you seem to have cooked up between you? Is he?'

'I don't know.' Marin suddenly found herself re-membering Jake's own phrase from that morning. 'We—we'll just have to cross that bridge when we come to it.' She took a deep breath. 'Please, Lynne, stop being angry and wish me well.'

'I'm not angry, just worried sick.' Lynne hugged her fiercely. 'And I think it would be better to wish you luck,' she added wryly. 'Because something tells me you're going to need it.'

She paused, frowning. 'A small point. What are you going to say to Barbara and Dad? You can't possibly tell them the truth.'

'I already spoke to them. We called them when we got back from Harborne.' She bit her lip. 'We let them think it was a whirlwind romance, and that we forgot everything but each other. At first they were really shocked and disapproving, but Jake managed to talk them round and although they're still a bit stunned, they're definitely coming to the wedding.'

'The spin doctor in action,' Lynne said bitterly. 'I'd better feed Mike the same story. I wouldn't want him to punch his future brother-in-law on the nose when they meet.'

'But there's one more thing you have to know,' Marin continued. 'Tomorrow I'll be moving out—going to live in Chelsea with Jake. Just for convenience sake,' she added hurriedly. 'It should have been tonight, but he said I was looking tired and that I'd been through enough upheaval for one day.'

She was expecting another explosion, but to her surprise, Lynne's lips quirked into a thoughtful smile.

'Then perhaps all hope is not lost,' she said, half to herself. Then, more briskly, 'Now, let's have a last girlie evening—supper in our dressing gowns and old movies on television. What do you say?'

Marin, her aching heart reminding her that hope had never existed in the first place, smiled and said, 'Wonderful.'

I don't like this room, thought Marin as she lay on the bed, gazing up at the ceiling. If I'm honest, I don't like this flat, either.

It was undeniably beautiful, of course. Probably the ultimate in contemporary chic. But it was cold in a way no amount of under-floor heating or mood-lighting could alleviate.

When she'd first seen it, she'd felt she was looking at a glossy still life painting. Something she could admire without wishing to own it, or respond to it emotionally.

Not that any kind of emotional engagement had been asked of her since she'd first come to live here ten long days ago, she reminded herself.

She was sharing a roof, she thought, with a polite stranger who had already left for the day before she awoke, and who returned just in time to join her for dinner in the evenings, after which he usually excused himself and went off to his study to work.

He was certainly keeping his side of the bargain, she admitted, but somehow that made her own situation no easier to bear. On the contrary.

But then everything about her stay here had been awkward, beginning with the moment when Jake had ushered her out of the lift carrying them up to the penthouse.

'I have a meeting in Canary Wharf, so I have to go,' he'd said, putting down her solitary suitcase. He'd smiled briefly at the tall, grey-haired woman who awaited them. 'But Jean—Mrs Connell—will look after you, and I'll see you tonight.'

He'd drawn her to him, dropped a kiss on her hair and gone.

'Welcome to Danborough Gate, madam.' Mrs Connell's tone was civil but for an instant her surprise showed on her face.

Clearly she'd been expecting a very different bride-to-be, someone glamorous and sophisticated, thought Marin, and tried not to mind.

'And may I take the opportunity to wish you every happiness?' the housekeeper continued, then paused, her expression faintly guarded. 'Mr Radley-Smith gave instructions for me to prepare the guest accommodation for you. Is that correct?'

'Yes,' Marin said quietly. 'Perfectly correct.'

I bet I'm the first female not to be shown straight to his bedroom, she thought without pleasure. She must really wonder what's happening, if he doesn't want to sleep with the girl he's going to marry.

Mrs Connell picked up the case and hesitated, clearly confused by its lightness. 'Is this all your luggage, madam?'

'Every scrap,' Marin returned.

Lynne, she reflected wryly, had gone through her wardrobe like the exterminating angel, leaving little but the clothing Jake had bought her for their weekend at Queens Barton.

'And even this won't fit you for long,' she'd commented as she'd packed. 'But, looking on the bright side, when you get your figure back you can stick him for a whole new trousseau. Won't that be great?'

'Fantastic,' Marin had said in a hollow voice.

Perhaps *fantastic* was the right word to describe everything that had happened to her, she thought now, remembering how she'd trailed round the flat in Mrs Connell's brisk wake, assimilating the large-reception rooms with their bleached, wooden floors, the three bedrooms—each with its own bathroom—the kitchen that looked like the flight deck on a spacecraft and the balcony, with its superb view of the river.

'There's also a very pleasant roof-garden, madam, which isn't overlooked by anyone, so it offers total privacy,' Mrs Connell had informed her. 'Mr Radley-Smith uses it a great deal.'

Which probably explains the all-over tan, thought Marin, her face warming. She focussed her attention hurriedly on a sunburst of white-and-gold flowers on a side table.

'How lovely,' she'd said. 'Did you arrange them?'

'Oh, no, madam.' Mrs Connell had shaken her head. 'We employ a floral art service. The young woman calls each Thursday.'

In addition to a previously mentioned laundry service and domestic-cleaning firm, Marin had

thought, startled. But if she'd wondered how Mrs
Connell—who seemed to arrive at dawn each day—
occupied her time when she had all this assistance,
she'd soon discovered that she was a magical cook.

It was also evident that Mrs Connell must have
had a confidential chat with Sadie, because all kinds
of little delicacies began suddenly to appear during
the day which Marin was not allowed to refuse.

Has no one told them that eating for two isn't
fashionable any more? she wondered, caught
between amusement and embarrassment.

But, apart from being pampered, she did not have
a great deal to fill her days. Mrs Connell's calm ef-
ficiency covered all eventualities at the house, Jake
had all the arrangements for the wedding in hand,
and once Marin had explained to an astonished
Wendy Ingram why she was no longer available for
work she'd found herself in a kind of limbo. Leaving
her, she realised, with far too much time to think.
And to fear the inevitable loneliness of the future.

Jake had arranged for her to visit the medical
practice he used, where she'd been received kindly
and cheerfully by Dr Gresham, one of the female
partners. Her examination had been gently reassuring, and she'd been told her general health was excellent.

'Although I'd be happier if you were less tense,'
the doctor had said at last. She'd given Marin a
searching look. 'You do want this baby, Miss Wade?'

'Yes,' said Marin. 'Oh, yes, I do. It's—very precious.'

And she knew that in spite of everything it was the truth, because it was all of the man she loved that she would ever have, or that she would be allowed to love and cherish openly without evoking ridicule or pity.

It's you and me against the world, little one, she thought, placing a protective hand on her stomach. Although from tomorrow, when your father transfers me to Harborne, that world may become slightly more bearable. And certainly more real.

Because the bedroom she'd been occupying was just like an ivory tower, she thought. Everything was in that same pale colour—the walls, the furniture, the bathroom tiles and fixtures and even the fabrics, apart from the vivid band of colour supplied by the crisply folded turquoise-and-gold coverlet making its own style statement from the foot of the bed.

And I, Marin told herself, make the place look untidy simply by being here.

Her mother, who'd been staying at Danborough Gate since her arrival from Portugal with Derek five days ago, had much the same thoughts.

'It's absolutely stunning, of course,' she'd said cautiously. 'Like a picture spread from some hideously expensive magazine. But it's not exactly home-like, certainly not somewhere you could leave a used cup or a newspaper lying around. And I can't imagine the kind of havoc a baby would wreak.

Although I would never say so to dear Jake,' she added hurriedly.

'He wouldn't be too disturbed,' Lynne had said, registering 'dear Jake' with an amused lift of an eyebrow. 'He calls it "the annexe"—a convenient extension to the office with great entertaining space.' She'd given Marin a mischievous look. 'A treat in store for you, honey, playing hostess.'

Marin had bitten her lip. 'I suppose so.'

Except it will never happen, she thought. Once the baby's born my duty's done, as far as Jake's concerned, and he won't want me back in London.

However, in the cause of neatness, she should really get up from the bed and put away her discarded wedding-dress, still lying where she'd thrown it in a sprawl of filmy, shell-pink lawn on the dressing stool.

It was a lovely dress and deserved better treatment, although it wasn't the kind of thing she'd ever intended to buy.

But Barbara had had her own ideas. She'd immediately vetoed Marin's half-hearted plan to buy a skirt and jacket which would have some indeterminate future use, and with Lynne's support had set off with her protesting daughter to trawl the boutiques.

She had tried in vain to persuade Marin into one of the enchanting creations in bridal white produced for their inspection but, when the soft cloud of high-waisted and ankle-length pink had emerged from its protective cover, she and Lynne had looked at each other and smiled in triumph.

So, even before the matching silk slip had slid over her head and down her still-slender body, Marin had known the decision was made.

It was far too romantic, she'd told herself with disquiet as she stared into the changing-room mirror, but that, of course, was what Barbara would expect.

After all, she'd been told that her shy daughter had been swept off her sensible feet into a passionate affair.

And her initial meeting with her future son-in-law, at his most charming, had totally confirmed that belief.

But then Jake's performance had been flawless throughout, Marin thought with a pang. He'd been warm, attentive and caring, with the occasional discreet hint of passion forcibly reined back.

And at the wedding this morning he'd produced a master stroke. It had been exactly the private, family occasion he'd promised, with Lynne and Mike acting as witnesses.

As Marin went to stand at Jake's side, she met his faintly questioning look with composure, agreeing to take James Anthony Radley-Smith as her lawful wedded husband in the steady tone which gave no hint of the hard knot forming in her chest.

But she faltered when she caught sight of the pair of gold wedding-rings lying on the cushion in front of them instead of just the single band she'd been expecting.

I thought it would be hypocritical to get married

in church, she thought numbly. Yet now he does this. *This*...

Her hand was shaking as Jake took the smaller ring, sliding it on to her finger. When it was her turn, she fumbled it, and his hand closed on hers, guiding her, pushing the gold band firmly over his knuckle and into place.

He looked down into her stormy eyes, his smile faintly crooked, then he bent and kissed her lightly and sensuously on the mouth.

It was over in an instant, but Marin felt the pressure of his lips curling in her bones and singing through her bloodstream.

Then, as she stood half-dazed, she heard laughter and applause and Barbara was hurrying forward, dabbing at her eyes, with Elizabeth, serene in lavender at her side, wanting to be the first to offer their own kisses and congratulations.

And throughout it all, Marin stood forcing herself to smile, while the words, 'What have I done? Oh God, what have I done?' whispered through her brain.

And they continued to prey on her mind while she picked at the magnificent poached salmon and accompanying array of salads Mrs Connell had prepared for the celebration lunch. She sipped at the half glass of champagne, which was all she was allowed, and listened to Derek's affectionate praise for her as he welcomed Jake to the family and proposed the health of the bride and groom. She tried not to notice the concern in Lynne's eyes, and Elizabeth Radley-Smith's faint frown.

It's a rite of passage, she told herself. A formality, like Jake saying just now how beautiful I looked today, and asking them all to drink to his wonderful wife. It's the done thing, and it will soon be over.

Lynne and Mike were the first to depart, then Elizabeth came to say goodbye. 'Although it should really be *au revoir.*' She paused. 'Sadie and the staff have gone into overdrive, making sure everything is perfection for your homecoming.' She added quietly, 'You're arriving on a wave of goodwill, Marin.'

Not I, thought Marin, but this tiny thing, barely a squiggle inside me. That's what really matters to everyone, and to Jake most of all, or this wedding would never have happened.

Barbara was tearful when the car arrived to take them to the airport. 'As soon as it's safe for you to fly, you're both coming out to stay; Jake's promised me. I'm so happy for you, darling,' she added huskily. 'It may have been rather quick, but I know you're in safe hands.'

'I wish I was coming to see you off.'

'Well, Jake's doing it for you.' Her mother paused. 'Besides, you're looking a little tired, my love. Why not have a nice rest while you wait for him to come home?'

An excellent notion, Marin thought drily, but impossible to carry out. She was too much on edge.

It was very quiet now. Mrs Connell had probably

finished restoring the place to its usual pristine condition as if nothing out of the ordinary had taken place there. And maybe it hadn't. Perhaps all today represented was a signature on a dotted line.

Look at it like that, she told herself. And deal with it.

The sudden rap on her door lifted her, startled, on to an elbow. Before she could speak, the door opened and Jake walked in, carrying a bowl of flowers—the cream roses, flushed with pink at their hearts, that he'd given her to carry at the ceremony.

'Jean thought you might like to have these,' he said without preamble. 'And she'll wrap the stems in damp cotton-wool tomorrow, if you want to take them with you.'

'Oh,' she said. 'That's—good of her. They're lovely.'

He set the bowl down on the dressing table and lifted the folds of pink lawn from the stool, letting them drift through his fingers. He said quietly, 'And so was this. You took my breath away.'

She was desperately conscious that she was wearing little more than a layer of silk. She said hurriedly, 'It wasn't really my choice—rather too Jane Austen.'

His brows lifted. 'You have a problem with Jane Austen?' he asked with faint amusement.

'Not at all,' she said. 'In normal circumstances.' She paused. 'Did Mummy and Derek get away all right?'

'Their flight was absolutely on time.'

'It was very kind of you to go with them, and to have them stay here.'

'It's been my pleasure,' Jake returned. 'Derek's a great bloke, and your mother's a honey.'

'And she seems to like you too.' Marin bit her lip. 'Which will make it all the harder for her when she realises that this marriage is a total fraud.'

'On the contrary, it was legally contracted before witnesses.' He held up his hand where the ring gleamed. 'Want extra proof?'

'An empty gesture,' she dismissed curtly.

'No,' he said. 'More a public statement that I'm off the market.' He added mockingly, 'I thought you'd be pleased.'

'No,' she said. 'You didn't.'

He shrugged. 'Then call it a whim.'

'And something else that you may live to regret.'

'Yes, indeed.' His mouth twisting, he dropped the dress back on the stool. 'Now, may we call a temporary truce and discuss supper? And, before you tell me you're not hungry, I saw how little you ate at lunch.' He paused. 'So, put something on and I'll make some scrambled eggs.'

'*You* will?' she queried incredulously.

'Why not?'

'I—I didn't know you could cook,' she returned lamely.

'Something else I picked up at university, where I was famous for my curried beetroot. However, I'm making the offer to feed you because Jean has made a tactical and tactful withdrawal for the rest of the day, leaving us quite alone to enjoy our wedding night.'

He paused, studying her reflectively, making her aware all over again of how little she was wearing. 'She probably thinks it's time my patience was rewarded.'

Her throat tightened. 'I hope that isn't a viewpoint you share.'

'No,' he said. 'Sadly, it is not.' The mockery was back in his voice, soft, insidious. 'So supper is quite safe, darling. You will not form part of the meal.' He glanced at his watch. 'Shall we say twenty minutes?'

He'd just started to beat the eggs when she arrived in the kitchen, punctual to the minute. He turned, his face expressionless as he surveyed the neutral sand-colour trousers and shirt she'd changed into.

Well, what was he expecting? she asked herself defensively. A black lace negligee?

'Do you want to eat here or in the dining room?'

'Here, I suppose,' Marin said, remembering ten days of stilted conversations across the other room's over-large table.

'As the lesser of two evils, by the sound of it.' Jake poured the eggs into a pan. 'You'll find cutlery and mats in that unit over there—second drawer.'

The eggs were perfect, served with rolls of crisply grilled bacon and a mound of buttered toast, and Marin discovered she was hungry after all.

'That was wonderful,' she told him when she'd eaten every scrap. 'You really can cook.' She gave him a mischievous look. 'But I'd rather not sample your curried beetroot.'

He grinned back at her. 'Nor would I, not again. It's a miracle I survived.

'I've also made coffee,' he went on as he put their plates in the dishwasher. 'Will you have some with me, or shall I fix you Ma's peppermint concoction?'

'I'll make myself some tea,' she said quickly. 'And take it to my room.'

'No,' he said. 'Have it here. I want to talk to you.'

'Talk about what?'

'I think marriage might qualify as a major topic.' Jake dropped a tea bag into a beaker and added boiling water, before pouring his own coffee. 'Don't you?'

Marin stared down at the cork mat in front of her. 'I think we've said all that's necessary already.'

'Then you wouldn't be prepared to reconsider the terms of our agreement?' he asked as he brought the drinks to the table.

She stiffened. 'What do you mean?'

He resumed his seat, looked down at his coffee. He said slowly, 'It's really quite simple. I want you to sleep with me tonight.'

'No.' Heart hammering unevenly, she pushed her beaker away, spilling some of the tea. 'No, of course not.'

His brows lifted. 'You speak with great conviction.'

'Because that's how I feel,' she said hoarsely. 'You have no right to ask that.'

'Then give me that right,' Jake said urgently. 'Darling, you're my wife, and we should at least try to make something of our life together.' He reached for her hand, which she snatched away. 'Come to bed with me and just let me hold you. I won't ask for more than that, I promise.'

'You think I'd believe any promise of yours—now?' She got to her feet, trembling. 'Yes, I made a fool of myself with you once, but that's over. As you agreed.'

She took a deep breath. 'I have your baby. In return, you leave me alone. That will never change. It can't.'

'Marin,' he said. 'Whatever regrets we had afterwards, we were happy together that night. I believe I could make you happy again—if you'd let me try.'

'Then keep to our agreement,' she said. 'And I'll be jubilant. But I won't sleep with you tonight or any other. I—I couldn't bear it.'

His chair scraped noisily across the tiles as he pushed it back from the table and rose. She flinched and saw the bitterness in his face turn to shock, and then a great weariness.

He said, 'Oh God, do you think—do you honestly imagine—that I'd...force you?' He shook his head. 'I simply hoped we might salvage something from this mess. Give this ludicrous marriage a chance. So I asked you a question. Now I've had my answer, and that's the end of it.'

He paused, the blue eyes cold. 'All the same, maybe you'd be wiser to take your tea to your room.'

He went on flatly, 'I'll be here tomorrow at midday to take you to Harborne. And you'll have the master suite there entirely to yourself. When I visit, I'll use my old room. That should put enough distance between us to reassure you.'

He added curtly, 'Now, goodnight.'

Marin left the beaker where it was and fled.

The bedroom ceiling hadn't changed much in the half-hour she'd been absent, she thought as she lay staring up at it once again.

No cracks had suddenly appeared in its smooth surface, threatening to bring the whole thing crashing down around her.

No, it was her life that lay in that kind of ruin, and she had brought it entirely on herself.

Oh God, she thought, shivering. Just for a moment, when we were laughing together in the kitchen, it felt so close, so right, like that other night all over again. And if he'd taken me in his arms then I'd have gone with him, given him anything—everything—that he asked.

But I need him to give in return. Because sex, however wonderful, can never be a substitute for the love I want from him. That I can't live without.

Let me hold you...

She turned over, burying her flushed face in the pillow, remembering what it was like to lie wrapped in his arms. To feel the strength of bone and muscle under her cheek, and breathe the scent of his skin.

There hasn't been a night, she thought with anguish, when I haven't remembered—haven't longed for him.

So why did I turn him away? Why couldn't I simply accept what was on offer and allow myself a little warmth to balance against all the chill to come? To armour me against the loneliness, when eventually he turns to someone else.

And, even if it's merely kindness again rather than passion, isn't that better than nothing, which is all I have now?

In a drawer she found a white silk-chiffon nightdress, still unworn, that Lynne had persuaded her to buy for Queens Barton.

She slipped it over her head, feeling the caress of the delicate fabric as it slid down her body.

In the shadows of the room, she looked as insubstantial as a ghost. But she was warm, living flesh and blood. A bride—a woman going to the man she loved.

Everywhere was in darkness as she went barefoot out into the passage, making her way to the room at the end.

She wouldn't say anything, she thought. She'd just slide into bed beside him, letting her presence speak for her. Offering him her willing surrender.

As she opened his door and slipped inside, she wondered if he'd be awake, finding sleep as elusive as she had herself.

The curtains were apart and the glow of the city lights outside illumined the room, revealing without mercy to her stunned gaze that the wide bed was empty, its covers undisturbed.

Telling her silently that the man who'd become her husband only that morning was spending his wedding night elsewhere—in all probability not alone.

And that their marriage was over even before it had begun.

CHAPTER TWELVE

'OF COURSE THERE'S going to be a party,' Elizabeth Radley-Smith declared firmly. 'Everyone in the locality is dying to meet you.'

'I'm not exactly a party person.' Marin bit her lip. 'Besides, is it really a good idea—under the circumstances?'

'You are Jake's wife,' Elizabeth returned. 'That's the only circumstance that matters.' She paused. 'Is he coming down this weekend?'

'No,' Marin said. 'Apparently not.'

'Indeed?' Her mother-in-law's tone was austere. 'And what reason did he give this time?'

'I didn't actually speak to him. His new PA called to give me the message.' *And I'm beginning to hate the sound of her voice.*

Watching Elizabeth begin to frown, Marin went on, improvising hastily. 'Lynne told me last week that the company is frantically busy. And Jake knows that I'm being well looked-after.' She made herself smile. 'Spoiled rotten, in fact.'

'Except that it should be Jake himself doing the spoiling,' Elizabeth returned drily.

I'm sure he is, thought Marin. Only somewhere else and with someone else.

But I can't let myself think about that or I might start to cry, and I only do that alone in bed at night.

Since her arrival at Harborne a month ago, she could count on the fingers of one hand the times that Jake had joined her there. His visits were generally concerned with estate business and lasted no more than overnight.

Nights that he spent well away from her in the bedroom he'd occupied since boyhood. Just as he'd said he would.

And, even if she'd ever been alone with him long enough to have the private conversation he seemed so anxious to avoid, what could she possibly have said? She couldn't think of a single question where she could risk hearing the answer.

Such as, 'Where did you go the night we were married?'

If there'd ever been a moment to ask, then maybe it was the following morning while they'd been driving down here. But, from the moment they'd come face to face, his aloof and devastating politeness had kept her silent. Warned her to remain so.

I turned him away, she thought. So, what did I expect—a vow of celibacy?

Elizabeth was speaking again. 'It would have been so much better if the two of you had gone off together after the wedding. Of course, it couldn't have been a honeymoon in the usual sense,' she added with faint embarrassment. 'But you might have been able to come to terms with the situation and each other. Maybe found a basis for friendship, at least.'

Friendship, Marin thought painfully. Could I have settled for that? Could I have taught myself to see him walk into a room, hear his voice and feel only mild pleasure instead of that joyous, agonised lift of the heart?

If he'd only been less kind and more cruel that first and only night—if he'd stepped back and told me it wasn't going to happen—yes, it would have hurt. Terribly. But I'd have recovered in time and got on with my life instead of being left to face a lifetime of regret, being with him and without him at the same time.

And obliged always to wonder...

Aloud, she said, striving for lightness, 'It's probably as well we didn't. I wouldn't have been very good company, being sick every day. I just hope it stops soon, and preferably this week, because I really need to go up to London.'

'Are you sure you feel up to that?' Elizabeth scrutinised her searchingly. 'You're looking rather too pale for my liking. When is your next doctor's appointment?'

'In a week's time,' Marin said. 'She wants to discuss booking me into the Martingdale Clinic for the birth. And I'm fine,' she added. *Apart, that is, from a severe case of unrequited love.* 'But I have to talk to the letting agents handling my flat. They wrote this morning to say my tenants have decided to go their separate ways, and are asking to do a deal over the remainder of the lease.'

And I'm the last person in the world to want them penalised for being unhappy.

She added, 'But I think my real decision is whether to re-let or sell up.'

'Then why don't I drive you up tomorrow?' Elizabeth suggested. 'I have some shopping to do, and we can meet for lunch later. The Casa Romagna, say, at one.'

Kindness clearly ran in the family, Marin thought wryly. Jake's mother was trying so hard to behave as if she had a real daughter-in-law that it would be churlish not to meet her halfway.

'I'd love that,' she said. 'But do you think we'll get a table? It's become incredibly popular since it won that award.'

'Oh, there are ways and means,' Elizabeth returned casually. 'So, shall I pick you up at nine-thirty?'

'It's a date,' said Marin.

When she was alone, she began her daily wander, the self-imposed ritual of moving slowly from room to room, running a hand over a favourite piece of furniture, adjusting the fall of a curtain, rearranging a cushion, gathering up the fallen petals of a flower, making it all her own, telling herself she belonged here and it was hers to care for in a way she'd never been tempted to do in Chelsea.

Sheer delusion on her part, of course. It was Jake's house and she was here purely on sufferance, keeping it in trust for the next generation.

She'd wondered how it would be with Elizabeth living so close, but even though the older woman came up most days to exercise her elderly gelding, Mr Gritty, she made these visits totally unobtrusive and was scrupulous about not dropping into the house uninvited.

Yet, in spite of the intrinsic awkwardness of their situation, there were plenty of invitations, because Marin enjoyed her company.

I meant to show her the paint cards for the nursery, she thought ruefully, *only she sidetracked me over this damned party. But it can't be held without a host, so all Jake has to do is find the projected dates inconvenient and the whole idea will simply die the death.*

The redecoration of the master suite was also becoming an issue, with books of fabric samples arriving almost daily at Sadie's behest.

The only trouble was the colour she liked best was a warm gold, almost identical to what was already there.

And Sadie's going to tell me it will fade just as badly, she told herself wryly. *But isn't that a small sacrifice to make in order to go on waking up in a room full of sunlight? Even if this time I'm alone there with just my memories.*

But she didn't feel particularly sunlit when she woke the next morning. She'd spent a restless night, and must have ended up lying awkwardly, because she had a niggling ache in her back.

For a moment she was tempted to call the London trip off and simply phone the agents. On the other hand, there'd be stuff to sign and Elizabeth's offer meant she didn't have to struggle with trains and the underground, while lunch at a top restaurant was appealing too. Besides, exercise might cure her niggle, she decided, easing herself off the mattress.

So she put on a plain mocha-coloured shift dress with matching low-heeled sandals, and was waiting, smiling resolutely, when the car drew up.

She did a little desultory but enjoyable window-shopping before making her way to the estate agency. An hour later she'd released her former tenants from any further obligations and agreed to put the flat on the market, spurred on by the information that potential buyers were already waiting to view.

Another bit of my life being dismantled, she thought as she hailed a cab to take her to Casa Romagna.

It was already frantically busy when she arrived ten minutes ahead of time, but a corner table was waiting, and the still mineral-water she asked for arrived almost at once.

The pain in her back hadn't vanished, as she'd hoped. If anything, it seemed to have become slightly worse, she realised, testing it with a cautious hand. But maybe Elizabeth would have something mildly analgesic in her bag that she could take.

She wasn't a great one for celebrity watching, but in a place like this it was almost irresistible, she decided, spotting in a ten-yard radius a well-known television presenter and the girl who'd won the award for best supporting-actress at the last Oscars.

Although if anyone looks at me, she thought, they'll be wondering 'Who the hell is that?'

Only to hear a woman's voice drawl, 'Well, if it isn't little Miss Wade herself.'

She glanced up with a sinking heart to see Diana Halsay standing beside the table.

'Except you're now Mrs Radley-Smith,' Diana went on, her mouth curling. 'And up the stick as well. Although I understand that wasn't the actual order of events.

'I was terribly upset not to be invited to the wedding, but I quite see why Jake preferred to keep it quiet.'

Marin put her glass down very carefully, feeling sick again. If I throw up, she thought, please God let it be all over her Jimmy Choos.

She said quietly, 'Good afternoon, Mrs Halsay.'

Diana's smile widened, became catlike. 'I hope you continue to think so. Because this really is the most amazing coincidence, finding you here today, when I'd heard that Jake had arranged to have you buried alive in the country and go his own merry way.

'You see,' she went on, 'I've just been talking about you to a former acquaintance of yours who simply can't wait to meet you again. You may remember I mentioned a friend who'd been doing up her house in the south of France? Well, here she is.'

She turned her head. 'Adela, darling, do come and say hello to the unblushing bride.'

No! The word seemed to explode in Marin's head. No, this can't be happening to me. It can't…

But Adela Mason was already sauntering towards them, immaculate in a fuschia-pink dress set off by a long, violet scarf.

'Well, well,' she said unpleasantly. 'You've certainly landed in clover, you treacherous little bitch. Diana tells me you've got your hooks into a millionaire, and that you've even managed to con him into marrying you to give your bastard a name.'

She hadn't bothered to lower her voice, and Marin could see heads turning at adjoining tables, looks being exchanged.

She had to say something, do something, she knew, but her skin felt clammy and the pain in her back was hurting her badly now, making it difficult to think of anything else, let alone speak.

'I hope the glamorous husband didn't insist on a pre-nuptial agreement,' Adela continued. 'Because he may not be pleased to learn that you're featuring in my divorce action. A starring role, no less. So you could find yourself out in the cold—big time. You, and your baby.'

She nodded. 'Yes, Greg and I are finished, and I'm blaming you, Marin Wade. You went after him, and you had him. And I'm going to make sure that your husband and everyone else knows what a dirty little slut you really are.'

Jake said quietly, 'Naturally, I'd be fascinated to hear what you have to say, but maybe you should start by telling me who you are.'

He was standing just a few feet away, his eyes glittering like blue ice, his mouth a grim line. Behind him was Elizabeth, her face appalled.

Adela swung towards him. 'My name is Mason,' she announced, raising her voice even higher. 'And a while ago I had the misfortune to employ this little tart as a typist. I thought *sex* was a word she couldn't even spell, until I found her rolling round naked with my soon-to-be ex-husband.

'No doubt she gave you the same treatment.' Her smile was contemptuous. 'Made you think butter wouldn't melt in her mouth, then jumped your bones. God, men can be so stupid.

'But it's not too late to wise up, even now. Spend some of your money having a DNA test done on the brat she's carrying. Find out who its real father is.'

Marin got to her feet. She was dimly aware of a crash as her chair fell over, of the faces all around studying her, avid, astonished. But, most of all, she saw Jake standing as if carved out of stone, all the colour draining from his face, looking at her with real horror in his eyes.

She wanted to defend herself, to tell him that everything Adela Mason had said was a vicious lie. That their baby was his and no one else's.

Instead, she heard herself say, 'Air—please, I need air.' Then the floor tilted and she felt something hit her head as she slid down into the pain-streaked darkness.

There was a bright light, but it wasn't the sun streaming through the curtains in her bedroom. It was too stark, too clinical for that.

And somewhere a voice was saying, 'Mrs Radley-Smith, wake up, dear.'

Her eyelids felt as if they had leaden weights attached but she forced them open obediently.

'That's better.' A strange woman was looking down at her, taking her wrist and checking the pulse.

But it didn't feel better.

Everything was white—the walls, the sheet that covered her, even the tunic and top the stranger was wearing. All white.

'Where am I?' Her voice was a croak.

'The Martingdale Clinic, dear.'

'No,' Marin said. 'That can't be right. That's next week. I'm sure it is.'

'Well, we're looking after you now instead.' The voice was professional and reassuring. 'So, lie quietly while I fetch the doctor to talk to you.'

She came back with a young man, curly haired and bespectacled.

He pulled forward a chair and sat down. 'How do you feel?' he asked quietly.

'My—head hurts.'

'I expect it does. You gave it quite a nasty crack when you fainted. That's why we're keeping you with us until we can be sure there's no concussion.'

'But it was my back that was aching,' she protested, adding slowly, 'Although that seems to have stopped now.'

'Yes.'

There was something about the way he said it that told her the truth.

She said, her voice a whisper, 'It was the baby, wasn't it? I've lost my baby.'

'I'm so very sorry. But please believe there was nothing to be done, even if you'd seen a doctor as soon as the pain started.' He paused. 'It's just one of those sad, unavoidable things, I'm afraid, and more common in these early months than you'd ever believe.

'It's no consolation, I know,' he added. 'But we've carried out the necessary procedures and it was all completely straightforward. You'll soon be as right as rain again.'

Marin lay very still staring at the blank, bland wall in front of her as memories began to filter back. A voice, she thought, saying foul, unforgivable things. Accusing her...

A man's blue eyes, bleak with shock and disbelief.

And she knew that nothing would ever be right again.

At last she said, 'Does—does my husband know about the baby?'

'Of course. He came with you in the ambulance. He's outside, waiting to see you.'

'No,' she said harshly, urgently. 'I don't want to. I can't. Make him go away.'

The doctor spoke gently, 'Mrs Radley-Smith, you've been through a miserable, traumatic experience, and that bang on the head hasn't helped. But your husband's had a bad time too, and he needs to reassure himself that you're all right.'

'Then tell him so,' she said. 'He'll believe you.'

He moved restively, 'But at a time like this you really need each other.'

'He doesn't need me,' she said. 'He's never needed me. It was the baby he wanted, only the baby, and now that's gone.' Her voice cracked. 'Everything's gone.' *And I don't belong here—not in this place where babies are born...*

'I'm sure you don't mean that.' His voice was awkward now, embarrassed at a situation he'd probably never encountered before. He frowned a little. 'But it's clear that you are very upset, so maybe visitors aren't the best idea right now.' He paused, adding reluctantly, 'I'll do as you ask and tell Mr Radley-Smith you're fine, but that you need to be left to rest quietly, and ask him to come back in the morning.'

It was a respite, she thought wretchedly when she was alone. But it would give her time to plan for a future that had suddenly changed beyond all recognition. And, above all, to think of a way that would set them both free from this non-existent marriage for ever.

Marin turned her face into the pillow and cried until she had no more tears left.

An hour or so later, the nurse returned with a large carrier bag bearing the logo of a top department-store.

'Your sister has brought some things in for you,' she announced. 'A nightie, some toiletries and a change of clothes.'

'Lynne's been here?' Marin sat up. 'Why did no one tell me?'

'I'm afraid the no-visitors rule applies to everyone once it's in place,' the older woman said in a faintly repressive tone. 'But she asked me to say that your mother has been contacted and will be flying in tomorrow.'

She paused. 'Also, we're moving you to a different room. One of our special suites. You have some lovely flowers waiting for you,' she added encouragingly. She took a tissue-wrapped, be-ribboned package from the carrier and extracted a pale blue silk nightdress and a matching *peignoir*. 'So, why don't I help you wash your face and hands and change, then we can get you tucked up for a nice rest before dinner? It's chicken in a cream sauce tonight.'

She kept up a flow of gentle chat while the transfer was being made.

The new room turned out to be special indeed,

more like an upgrade in a top hotel, Marin thought wryly.

Everyone seemed to have sent flowers—Elizabeth, Lynne and Mike, Sadie and the staff at Harborne, and Mrs Connell. And in the centre of them all was an enormous basket of cream roses flushed with pink, like her wedding bouquet, with a card saying simply, 'Jake.'

As she looked at them, smelled their perfume in the air, she thought of her wedding night. Of the humiliation of going to his room—his empty bed—to offer herself, and knew she could not risk that happening to her again.

She ate some supper, and after the doctor's visit watched a little television, then accepted the hot milk with honey and nutmeg that the nurse brought to help her sleep.

Then she lay awake, staring into the darkness with eyes that burned as she worked out what to do, what to say, to bring the pain and unhappiness of the past weeks to a close.

She'd expected Jake to be at the clinic before they'd finished serving breakfast, but it was nearly midday when he eventually arrived, bringing Barbara with him. Marin welcomed her with trembling lips and tears in her eyes, and was glad when Jake left them alone together.

Hugged, comforted and the medical details dealt with, Marin took a deep breath. 'When I get out of here, could I come and stay in Portugal with you and Derek for a while?'

'Of course, darling.' Barbara stroked her hair. 'But can Jake get away?'

'I was thinking I'd come on my own.'

'Oh.' Barbara was silent for a moment. 'Are you quite sure about that?'

'Yes, why not?'

'Because, darling, Jake's your husband,' her mother said levelly. 'He has a right to be consulted about your plans. And he may have some of his own for when you're better. That honeymoon you never had, for instance.'

She patted Marin's hand. 'It used to be said that as soon as you recovered from a miscarriage you should try for another baby.' She sighed. 'But I expect the medical profession now takes a different view.'

'Yes.' Marin felt as if a leaden weight had settled in her chest. 'I'm sure they do.'

And anyway I can't—*can't*...

'So talk the Portugal idea over with Jake,' Barbara went on. 'And we'll get things fixed up.' She lowered her voice. 'He arranged for me to fly over first class, you know. The ticket was waiting at the airport. Wasn't that wonderful?'

Marin nodded. She said with an effort, 'He is— very kind.' *But I can no longer live with that kindness. And somehow I have to tell him so.*

He came slowly into the room and walked across

to the bed, standing looking down at her, his mouth set, his eyes shadowed.

He said gravely, 'How are you feeling?'

'I think the stock response is "as well as can be expected."' She swallowed. 'About the baby...I—I'm so sorry.'

'Don't say that,' he said quietly. 'You must never say that. Things happen, and for all kinds of reasons. And it's no one's fault.'

'No—well.' She looked away. 'Thank you for bringing my mother over.'

'It was no problem,' he said. 'But it wasn't altogether altruistic, either.' His tone was ironic. 'I thought my presence here might be more acceptable if I didn't come alone.'

Marin flushed. 'What do you mean?'

'Don't play games, darling. The doctor's obvious embarrassment when he made your excuses yesterday spoke volumes. You didn't want to see me.'

'I'm surprised you wanted to see me,' she said in a low voice. She made herself look at him. 'You may not believe it after the things Adela Mason said, but the baby was yours, Jake.'

His brows lifted. 'Why would I doubt it?'

'I saw the expression on your face when she was screaming her lies. You looked horrified.'

'How was I supposed to look?' he asked. 'When my pregnant wife suddenly started losing our baby? All I thought about was getting you to hospital.' He shrugged. 'As for Diana and her unpleasant friend, if they told me April followed March I'd check a calendar.'

He paused. 'Anyway, I already knew what had happened in France.'

'How?'

'I couldn't figure how you'd ended up in London homeless and jobless, so I asked Lynne.' He smiled faintly. 'You're hardly anyone's idea of a home-wrecker. Besides,' he added drily, 'I knew what those two witches could never know—that you were a virgin when I made love to you.'

She said, 'Oh,' then looked down, aware that her face was burning.

There was a silence and his gaze took in the demure lines of the blue nightgown. 'That colour suits you.'

'As you once said, Lynne has very good taste.' She played with the edge of the sheet. 'Please will you make sure she's reimbursed for all the lovely things she bought? She must have spent a small fortune.'

'Yes,' Jake said, after a pause. 'I'll see to it.' He added, 'I'm going to ask the doctor if I can take you home later today.'

She said quickly, 'I'm not sure he'll agree. I'm still getting headaches from my fall.' She paused. 'Besides, my mother has said that when I leave the clinic I can go back to Portugal with her, and I'd really like to do that. If you have no objection.'

'I'm not likely to object to anything that will help you recover,' he said slowly. 'Of course you may go, if that's what you wish.'

'But that isn't all.' She took a deep breath. 'When I come back, I want us to get a divorce.'

There was another more profound silence, then he said quietly, 'What the hell are you talking about?'

'About our lives,' she said huskily. 'The future. After all, we only got married for the baby's sake. And if we hadn't been in such a hurry, if we'd waited just a few more weeks, there'd have been no need for us to be married at all.

'Everything that's happened between us has been so wrong,' she went on quickly. 'But now we have a chance to put it right and begin again. Get our real lives back and make a fresh start. No more pretending for either of us.'

Jake turned away and walked over to the window. Staring down into the street outside, he said, 'You seem to have thought this out very thoroughly.'

'Our lives have changed completely. It's been a good time to think,' Marin said, keeping her voice steady. 'You had no intention of sleeping with me that night. You said as much. And marrying me was simply the honourable thing to do.' She paused. 'Because you can't ever have imagined the kind of empty relationship we've stumbled into.'

'No.' His attention was still fixed on the view from the window. 'I grant you that.'

'And one of these days you'll meet someone you can't resist,' she went on swiftly. 'And you'll settle down and have a real wife—a real family. Give Harborne its next generation.'

'It's good of you to take such an interest in my welfare.' He turned then, surveying her, hands on hips. 'But what about you, Marin? I hope our mutual nightmare hasn't put you off for ever. That you'll marry again too.'

'Yes,' she said. 'Of course. In time.'

'Which leaves me little to say, except I won't fight you over the divorce—and I wish you luck.'

'Thank you,' she said.

And thank God, she thought, that I did all my crying last night. That I can do this, say this to him, without breaking down and giving myself away.

'However,' Jake went on. 'It might be better not to mention our plans to other people just yet. I don't think they would understand the timing.'

She moved restively. 'We could always say that my trip to Portugal gave us the chance to think. To admit we didn't have a future.'

'How very practical of you, darling.' He smiled. 'I can tell everyone that your absence made me realise how much I enjoyed being single.'

'And I'll say I decided that I can be happy again too.' She smiled back resolutely. 'So—sorted!'

'Completely.' He walked back to the bed. 'Shall we spare each other the usual meaningless nonsense of remaining good friends?'

She didn't look at him. 'I don't think we were ever that.'

'Probably not,' he conceded. 'And the Chelsea flat is yours for the duration,' he added abruptly. 'Your

mother is staying there, naturally, and I'll make sure
I'm around as little as possible until you both leave
for Portugal.'

Her eyes flew to his face. 'But you?' she asked.
'Where will you go?'

He said quite gently, 'I don't think that's any of
your business, sweetheart. Do you?'

And he went.

CHAPTER THIRTEEN

'JAKE TELEPHONED WHILE you were in the village.' Barbara said as Marin walked into the kitchen. 'Asking what flight you'd be catching tomorrow.'

Marin's heart gave a sudden lurch. 'Why should he want to know that?' She put the shopping basket on the table and began to unpack it.

Her mother's brows lifted. 'So that he can meet you at the airport, I presume,' she said with faint tartness. 'It's hardly surprising when he hasn't seen you for over a month.' She sighed. 'Such a shame that he couldn't get away and join you here after all.'

Marin took out a punnet of grapes, stared at it then put it back in the bag. The moment of truth seemed to have arrived, she thought wretchedly, and there was no point in prevaricating any longer.

She said, 'Actually, it isn't quite as simple as that. When I return to London, I'm getting a divorce.'

One of the pottery mugs Barbara was lifting down from a shelf crashed to the tiled floor and broke into a dozen pieces.

Mother and daughter looked at each other across the fragments, then Barbara said, 'Have you gone quite mad? Is that bang on the head still affecting you?'

'On the contrary,' Marin returned. 'I've made a perfectly sensible and rational decision to end a marriage that should never have begun and now has no reason to continue.'

'Oh, for God's sake,' Barbara said impatiently. 'What in the world has common sense to do with being in love?'

Marin turned away. 'But we're not in love. We only pretended to make the whole thing seem—less sordid, I suppose.'

There was a silence. Then Barbara said quietly, 'Are you trying to tell me that you went to bed—conceived a child—with a man you cared nothing for?' She shook her head. 'Oh, Marin, nothing would ever make me believe that.'

Marin bit her lip. 'I'm sorry, but it happened. He was glamorous and exciting, and I—behaved badly. For which I have no possible excuse. I—I'm deeply ashamed.'

'Ashamed of being human?' Barbara asked. 'Oh, darling.'

'Ashamed of behaving like the worst kind of fool,' Marin returned. 'But at least I can put things right now, before any more damage is done.'

Barbara fetched a dustpan and began clearing up the broken china. She said gently, 'Marin, you cannot end a marriage as if you were taking back a dress that didn't fit. And what about Jake? How does he feel about this? Or haven't you told him yet?'

'On the contrary, we're in complete agreement. There's no question of any financial settlement,' Marin added quickly. 'He's bound to offer, but I want nothing from him. Just—a clean break.'

She drew a determined breath. 'I shall be going back to work at the agency, and I've taken my flat off the market, so I have a job and somewhere to live. That's all I need.'

There was a silence, then Barbara said, 'I noticed, of course, that you weren't wearing that beautiful ruby he gave you, but I thought perhaps that you'd had to remove it—something to do with hospital regulations.'

Marin shook her head. 'It's an heirloom. Naturally, I'm going to return it.'

'Quick and painless.' Barbara's voice was clipped as she emptied the contents of the dustpan into the bin. 'And you really think you can just as easily eliminate the last few months—your husband—from your life as if they'd never existed and emerge unscathed? Dream on.'

Marin stared at her. 'You speak as if you're on Jake's side.'

'I'm on the side of "think again before you really mess up your life",' Barbara retorted vigorously.

'But that's exactly what would happen if I stayed with Jake.' She paused. 'I'm sorry. You liked him, didn't you?'

'Derek and I both did.'

Marin forced a smile. 'And you thought he was attractive, didn't you, Ma? Confess.'

'Yes, I did, not being in my dotage. Who wouldn't?' Her mother paused. 'But it's not just his attraction, Marin. I've been married to two wonderful but very different men, but neither of them would have dreamed of going into a women's department and buying me a complete set of clothing from the skin out.'

'But Lynne bought those things,' Marin protested.

'She delivered them to the clinic,' Barbara agreed. 'But everything in those bags Jake chose and paid for. Including that heavenly blue nightdress and robe.'

'Oh.' Marin bit an already sore lip. 'Then why did he let me think it was Lynne?'

Barbara took down two more beakers and filled them with coffee from the pot on the stove.

'Well, darling, that hardly matters, does it?' she said, her tone almost casual as she handed one to her daughter. 'Not when you're getting a divorce. So you'll never know, now. Will you?'

She paused again. 'And such a pity about that lovely ring,' she added almost inconsequentially. 'I read somewhere once that rubies are supposed to be a symbol of love, bringing contentment and peace. But not, it seems, for you, darling.' She sighed. 'What a shame. What a terrible shame.'

* * *

Marin was on edge throughout the flight the next day. For the first time ever, she realised she'd been almost glad to leave the villa and return to the UK.

The previous evening had been an awkward occasion. Derek had clearly been told about the state of her marriage and, trying to be tactful, had talked about everything else under the sun.

She'd excused herself early, saying she had to finish packing, but that hadn't been strictly true. In reality, she'd needed to pick out something else to wear for the journey, because putting on the silky skirt and top in dark honey that Jake had chosen for her had become a total, heart-wrenching impossibility.

In fact, she could never wear them again, she thought, her throat closing as she remembered how the bias-cut skirt had rippled round her legs as she'd walked out of the clinic to the waiting car, and how the deep, rich colour, like captured sunshine, had warmed her skin and in some strange way made her feel less sad. Less hopeless.

And he'd bought it for her, together with that set of incredibly pretty lace-edged underwear, even managing to get her cup-size correct, she thought, feeding her resentment that he should be aware of so many intimate details about her when she didn't even know where he purchased his elegant shirts.

But I never wanted to know, she told herself. Because it was all part of keeping my distance. Of turning him into a stranger so that I could avoid being hurt too badly. And how did I ever think it could possibly work?

Certainly not when she was unable to forget the way his hand had once cupped her breast as if that had been the sole purpose of its creation, or how his body had filled hers with such magnificent completion.

But for the sake of her own sanity she had to try, so she'd buried the honey silk at the bottom of her case and pulled out a taupe linen skirt and white tee-shirt instead.

At some point, she realised unhappily, she would have to arrange the collection of the rest of her clothes and personal things from Harborne. Or perhaps Elizabeth would have them sent to her.

Now, as she made her way through customs and out into the arrivals area, she felt cold with tension in case Jake really had come to meet her. But awaiting her instead was the same impersonal car and driver who'd delivered her to the airport the previous month.

As she settled into the luxury of the backseat, Marin tried hard to tell herself that the mixed feelings inside her were actually relief.

Besides, she told herself with resolution, very soon she'd be back in her own flat, and that was bound to help. Work was what she needed, and familiar routine. A chance to 'move on.'

Lynne, nobly refraining from asking the obvious questions, had agreed to leave basics like milk, bread and coffee for her. Tomorrow she'd do a big shop, but tonight she'd order in—pizza, probably, from the place round the corner. It didn't matter much.

She hadn't eaten on the flight, so she should be hungry, but she wasn't. Just chilled and bleak, as if she would never be warm again.

The flat felt chilly too, and somehow smaller. No doubt because she'd got too used to Chelsea and Harborne, she told herself scathingly as she dumped her case in the bedroom. Time to come down to earth.

Lynne, she discovered gratefully, had made up her bed and switched on the immersion heater, while the fridge had also been stocked with bacon, eggs and orange juice.

There was even a bowl of freesias on the coffee table, with a card saying 'Welcome back, L and M.'

The only thing missing was the spare latchkey which Lynne had forgotten to leave behind. But in the broad scheme of things that hardly seemed important.

Marin looked round the living room, wondering whether to unpack and load the washing machine or dig out the folder with the takeaway menus, and found that neither option held much appeal.

It was easier just to stand, waiting for this, her real home—her only home—to welcome her back. To close round her and hug her. To stop her feeling so lost and alone.

But at the moment it seemed in no hurry to do so.

The departing tenants had taken good care of it, but all the same it felt—almost alien. As if she no longer belonged there.

I'm just tired, she thought. Maybe I should concentrate on getting a good night's sleep and pick up on my life tomorrow. Things will seem better then.

She was in the bedroom, kneeling to unlock her suitcase, when she heard her front door open and close quietly.

Lynne, she thought, probably returning that damned key. But please, *please,* let her not ask too many questions. Not this evening. Because I don't think I can take it.

She called, 'I'm in here.'

'So I see,' said Jake.

He stood in the doorway, immaculate as always in dark navy pinstripe, a leather traveling-bag in one hand and a suit-carrier slung over his shoulder. He was smiling faintly, and Marin felt her whole body clench in a physical response as instinctive as it was reluctant to the unwelcome force of his attraction.

His blue gaze scanned her. 'You're looking well. A tan suits you.'

'I—I'm fine,' she returned, scrambling to her feet. 'How did you get in?' Her voice was uneven, husky. A betrayal if ever there was one, she thought, cursing inwardly.

'With this, of course.' He held up the missing key. 'Lynne gave it to me.'

'Oh,' she said, and took a deep, steadying breath.

'Well, thank you, but it could easily have waited. Lynne shouldn't have asked—shouldn't have brought you out of your way—just for a key.'

He shrugged. 'It's not a problem.'

'Well,' Marin said tautly. 'You mustn't let me keep you. You're obviously going somewhere.'

'On the contrary,' Jake returned. 'I've just arrived.'

She pointed to the bags. 'Are those my clothes from Harborne?'

'No,' he said. 'They're mine from Danborough Gate.'

He looked past her to the bed made up with its pristine white linen and coverlet.

'How very pure,' he commented sardonically. 'Trying to regress back to virginity, darling?' His smile widened. 'I doubt that's possible, even if you wanted to.

'And only one pillow,' he added softly. 'Now, that is real togetherness.' He walked over to the fitted wardrobe and opened the door, revealing the empty hanging-rail.

'I'll take the right-hand side,' he said. 'Unless you have any objections.'

'Objections?' Marin's voice was shaking. 'Of course I have objections. What is this? What the hell do you think you're doing here?'

'Moving in,' he said, laconically. *Mi casa, su casa* stuff.' He glanced round him. 'It's all pretty compact, admittedly, but that means less room for you to run and hide, which is a distinct advantage.

And even better,' he added softly. 'We'll be completely alone together, just as if we were on honeymoon.'

She stared at him, shock sending her pulses crazy. 'What—what are you talking about?'

'Marriage, of course,' he said. 'But the real thing this time, Marin. We really are going to stop pretending, my sweet, just as you claimed you wanted.'

'But it's over.' The words were almost a wail. 'We're getting divorced. We agreed.'

'Ah, the divorce,' he said softly. He was removing suits and shirts from the carrier and hanging them up. 'That isn't going to happen—at least, not yet.'

'You said you wouldn't fight it,' she accused, her voice rising. 'Oh God, I should have known I couldn't trust you.'

'Your battle is with the legal system, darling,' Jake retorted. 'You see, we haven't been together long enough to qualify for divorce. The law requires us to have been married for a whole year, and as you know we've never really been married at all, not in the strict sense of the word.

'Which,' he added, almost casually, 'is something I intend to put right without delay.'

He sent her another swift smile. 'However, when the year is up, we can talk again about divorce—if you still want to. But I reserve the right to try and persuade you to change your mind in the meantime.'

She lifted her chin. 'Presumably,' she said coldly. 'This is a joke?'

'No,' he said. 'I couldn't be more serious.'

'It's revenge, then.' Her breathing quickened. 'Because I made it clear I don't want you, my homecoming has to be ruined.'

'It's not that, either,' he said. His glance was faintly sardonic. 'And I think the level of our mutual desire has yet to be established.

'Ah,' he went on as the doorbell sounded. 'That should be dinner arriving: steaks, salad, cheese, fruit and some good Bordeaux. Shall we toss a coin to decide who's in charge of the grill?'

'That won't be necessary.' Marin told him defiantly. 'I'm having pizza.'

He shrugged. 'Then I'll cook for myself. It's no hardship.'

He went into the hall and Marin followed, watching him receive a wicker hamper and hand over a generous tip before she hurriedly escaped to the living room.

She was standing by the window, her arms folded across her rigid body, when Jake rejoined her. He'd discarded his jacket and tie and unbuttoned his waistcoat, and his shirt was open at the throat.

He looked totally relaxed, whereas she felt as if she was strung up on wires.

'Feel this is safer territory than the bedroom?' he asked. His gaze travelled to the comfortably cushioned sofa. 'I wouldn't count on it.' He slanted a lazy grin at her. 'As you, my sweet, would have soon discovered if I'd been allowed to date you—court you, as I originally planned. And you have a nice, soft hearthrug too. Excellent.'

'Please,' Marin said unsteadily. 'Please don't do this—say these things. Don't make matters worse than they already are. Just leave.'

'Well, I considered it,' he said slowly. 'When we lost our baby and you behaved as if the only link between us had been cut, and you didn't want me anywhere near you ever again, not even to grieve with you. It occurred to me then that maybe I should do the decent thing and go. Get out of your life, if that was all that would make you happy.

'Only then I started thinking very selfishly about how unhappy it would make me. That maybe I didn't want to be airbrushed out of the picture. To have my marriage junked before it had even begun.'

He had the gall to smile at her again. 'After all, I needed something to keep me at home in the evenings, and stamp collecting has never appealed, so you seemed the obvious answer.'

'This,' Marin said shakily, 'is no laughing matter.'

'No,' he said with sudden, aching bitterness. 'But then, we haven't really laughed for a long time, have we? Not since that one, solitary night we spent together. We laughed then, kissed, touched. And you lay in my arms and held me as if you would never let me go. I felt as if I'd been shown paradise.

'Only then, in the morning, I was suddenly a pariah—an outcast—and our perfect night just a ghastly mistake committed because you were drunk—unbalanced—under the illusion I was some-one else.

'Any excuse would do, it seemed. Any bloody stupid reason to deny that you'd been my woman in every blessed, wonderful way there was. That we belonged to each other and we always would.'

The blue gaze was suddenly fierce. 'And that's why I'm not leaving, Marin. Because I want her back—the sweet, wild, generous girl who came into my arms and gave herself so completely that I told myself it had to be the love I'd hoped and prayed for.'

He took a deep, uneven breath. 'Because I want you, my darling—rich or poor, sick or well—for the rest of my life. I want us to make a home together, and in spite of this recent sadness, have a family one day. I want the right to say to people, "I don't think you've met my wife".'

He stopped. 'Oh God, sweetheart, you're crying; that's the last thing I intended to happen.' He came to her, drawing her over to the sofa and sitting beside her. 'Is it really so impossible for you to find some happiness with me? Is that what you're trying to say?'

Marin choked back a sob. 'Jake, you don't mean it. You can't.' She looked down at the hands clasping hers. 'You don't want to be married to anyone. You never have, and the only reason you're saying these things now is probably because you're feeling sorry for me again—and, if so, I—I can't bear it.'

'Sorry for you?' There was incredulity in his voice. 'What in hell are you talking about?'

'I'm talking about me,' she said raggedly. 'Me—making a complete fool of myself over you at Queens Barton and everyone seeing and laughing at me.

'Me—throwing myself at you in the bedroom that night, although I realised—your whole attitude said—that you didn't want me.'

'Marin.' His voice was infinitely gentle. 'What happened between us was totally down to me, because I couldn't resist kissing you—touching you—even though I'd been trying so hard to behave well for once.

'Because I wanted a life with you, darling, not an affair. I wanted us to make love to each other because we were in love. Mutually. Irrevocably.'

He gave an uneven laugh. 'As it was, I'd been watching you all evening. Waiting for the moment when I could ask you to dance—have a legitimate excuse to hold you, if only for a few minutes. But you said no. Something I told myself I would have to get used to.

'So do you know what I was doing just before you asked me to fix your zip? I was having a cold shower—reminding myself in a pretty basic way that sex was definitely not on the agenda, even if you were spending another night only a few yards away from me.'

He paused. 'And what do you mean, people were laughing at you? Because I understood I was the weekend's chief object of derision.'

'It was Diana,' she said in a low voice. 'She saw me the next morning and guessed what had happened. Said vile, horrible things. Told me she knew you weren't really involved with me, but that I'd obviously started to believe it, and—and to want you. And that, when you realised, you'd taken pity on me.'

'And you believed her?' His tone was incredulous.

She bent her head. 'Yes,' she said. 'Because I knew that what she said was true. That you'd never been going to touch me until I begged you.'

'Christ,' he said softly. 'She really is the ultimate bitch. With her unerring instinct for the jugular, she told me everyone was enjoying watching me trail around after you like a beaten dog. That I'd made myself a total laughing stock.'

She stared at him, lips parted in shock. 'What did you say to her?'

Jake produced a handkerchief and blotted the remaining tears from her face. He said ruefully, 'Well, I could hardly deny it, either, sweetheart. So, I thanked her for her interest, said we would always be grateful to her for bringing us together but that we would quite understand if she felt unable to attend the wedding.'

She swallowed. 'You said that?'

He said with feeling, 'Believe me, that was the easy part. Convincing you that my ultimate intentions were completely honourable turned out to be something else again.'

She looked down at the floor. 'But you only asked me to marry you because I was pregnant.'

'No,' he said. 'That just moved everything forward by a few months. Besides, I didn't think you'd agree on any other terms. And if I'd told you the truth—that I'd always intended marriage, and the baby was a bonus—would you have believed me? Be honest.'

She swallowed. 'Probably not.'

'That's what I thought.' His tone was wry. 'After all, you'd made it more than clear that our night together had been some kind of horrifying aberration. And then you vanished without a word.'

He shook his head. 'But I never considered Diana as a reason for your change towards me. I blamed myself entirely, because there'd been times that night when I'd almost forgotten it was your first time with a man, and I was left wondering if I'd asked too much—disgusted you in some way.'

His mouth twisted. 'A nightmare that seemed totally confirmed when you told me you wanted us to sleep apart after the wedding.'

'Because I thought you didn't love me,' Marin said in a low voice. 'I couldn't forget what Diana had said. I was terrified you'd be having sex with me out of duty, or worse still pity. Or that I might end up—pleading again. I decided it was better to be alone. Then at least I'd have some pride left.'

'I have news for you,' he said. 'There isn't much room for pride when you love someone.'

'I know that.' She was silent for a moment. 'On our

wedding night, I went to your bedroom to find you, to tell you I'd changed my mind about sleeping with you. But you weren't there.' She hesitated again. 'I probably have no right to ask, but where did you go?'

'Not very far,' he said. 'Just back to the kitchen, sitting in the dark, making the intimate acquaintance of a bottle of scotch and wondering how I would ever cope with the hell of loneliness I'd made for myself. How I was going to live without even the hope of an occasional cuddle.'

She swallowed. 'Jake, darling, I don't have any illusions about myself. I know the kind of girls that you've spent time with in the past, and I'm not one of them.'

He cupped her face in his hands, looking down into her eyes with such tenderness that her heart skipped a beat.

'My sweet, the need to kiss you—make love to you—is nearly driving me crazy. So let me make a few things clear while I can still think straight.

'You said earlier that I never wanted to be married. That's not true, but I had a hard act to follow. My parents fell in love when they met, and they were lovers all through their life together— something that embarrassed the hell out of me during adolescence.

'But later, when I grew up and acquired some sense, I realised I wanted what they had and nothing less would do.'

He added quietly, 'Ma's a terrific woman, but when Dad died it was as if a light inside her had been switched off.

'But I never found anyone who came near turning on that same light for me—in fact, I'd pretty much given up hope, until I walked into the company flat looking for Lynne and found you instead, wearing nothing but a bloody towel, and spitting at me like an angry cat.'

Her lips parted in a silent gasp. 'Are you saying you fell in love with me then?'

'At the time,' Jake said carefully, 'I was rather more interested in figuring if I could get you out of that towel and purring like a kitten instead. It was only later, at the reception, that I realised what was really happening to me, when I told Diana we found each other and knew it was the absolute truth.'

He shook his head. 'God, you were so amazing that evening, smiling at complete strangers and talking to them, trying your hardest not to seem shy, behaving as if being with me was what you really wanted. I spent my time longing to pick you up in my arms and keep you safe and loved for ever.'

He added flatly, 'I didn't want to accept Graham's invitation down to Queens Barton because I knew it meant all kinds of trouble. But I decided the chance of a couple of days with you was too good to miss. That I could spend them at least trying to get you to like me a little better.

'I thought, too, on the way home I'd take you to

Harborne. I wanted to see you there—the girl I loved, in the house I loved. Our future home.'

Marin's eyes widened. '*That* was the detour you mentioned?'

He nodded. 'I'd already told my mother her prayers had been answered and I'd found my future wife, and I knew she'd be dying to meet you.' He paused. 'Only then I behaved like an impatient, sex-mad idiot and wrecked everything for us. Told myself I'd forfeited any chance of persuading you to fall in love with me in return. That instead I'd given you every cause to hate me.'

'All the time we were apart,' she whispered, 'I never stopped thinking about you—wanting you. But I daren't call it love. And I told myself that the best way to cure myself was to make sure I never saw you again. That eventually, somehow, I'd forget.'

'God, what a pair of fools we've been,' Jake said huskily. 'And I might still be stumbling round like a zombie, telling myself that my life was over, but for our female relations.'

'What do you mean?' His arm was round her now and she was nestling against him, feeling the warmth of him permeating her entire being, driving out the bleak chill within her. Filling her with a new radiance.

'Your mother.' He kissed her forehead. 'Telling me in every phone call to Portugal that you were missing me.

'My mother.' He kissed the tip of her nose.

'Saying she'd seen the way you looked at me sometimes when you thought no one was watching.

'And, of course, Lynne.' His mouth brushed hers, gently and sweetly. 'Who argued from the first that I wasn't that bloody irresistible, and as you didn't believe in casual sex you'd never have given yourself unless it meant something to you too.

'Small foundations for hope, perhaps, but I was desperate. And it made me realise there was no way I was going to give up on you or our marriage. That I'd fight and go on fighting until all hope was gone.'

Marin slid her arms round his neck, feeling the race of his heartbeat against hers.

'But now the war's over.' She smiled up at him, all barriers swept away, her eyes shining with new-found confidence and the glorious, brimming delight of being free to offer him her entire self. To take him as her husband at last. 'So why, my darling, don't we make love instead?'

Jake got to his feet, the blue eyes caressing her hungrily as he lifted her up into his arms.

He said softly, 'I thought you'd never ask.' And carried her away to where their bed waited.